the art of avoiding your soulmate

WILDWOOD

LOLA GLASS

Cover by Francesca Michelon
https://www.merrybookround.com/

To new changes
And sarcastic banter

one

SIENNA

THE COUNTRY MUSIC playing from the artfully-western bar's jukebox was driving me crazy, but I ignored it.

Again.

Because the pack's ladies had convinced me to go out with them, and like the sucker I was, I didn't have the balls to say no.

Spoiler: I never had the balls to say no.

Even though I knew they would introduce me to a few more guys that the alphas in town had decided could potentially be my mate.

Anyway, it was becoming a serious problem. They made a *lot* of plans, and I was so damn tired of being sported around like some old-fashioned human girl looking for a husband.

Sometimes, I just needed to take a long shower and pretend I wasn't a living, breathing person.

I was, of course.

A living, breathing blood wolf, to be exact.

Both vampire and wolf.

We were created to act as living blood bags for vampires, which was a shitty way to live. And may have contributed somewhat to my yes-man tendencies.

But it was what it was.

So I needed to make the best of it.

...By learning how to say no, probably.

I lifted my glass of water off our table, taking a sip. Before my parents had overdosed and lost their lives when I was a kid, I'd seen them addicted to anything and everything, so I didn't touch alcohol or drugs with a hundred-foot pole.

Three of the other five girls with me were out on the makeshift dance floor, which I had narrowly dodged being dragged out to. The other two were in a heated discussion about the best way to cook steak.

My phone buzzed, and I glanced down. There was a message from one of my two best friends—both of whom were the only other blood wolves I knew. Our group chat got plenty of use.

Love was mated to the alpha of the pack that ran the city. It was called the Wildwood Pack, which the city was named after.

Tori was mated to the alpha of a tiny pack of government wolves. They traveled fairly often, but the outskirts of Wildwood was their home base.

TORI

How many guys have they introduced you to tonight?

ME

Only two, but the night is still young.

LOVE

Any excuses in sight?

ME

Unfortunately, no

TORI

Just tell them I'm sick and you need to take care of me

ME

You're a blood wolf. You don't get sick

TORI

They don't know that

ME

Pretty sure Vex doesn't want me spreading word that he can't take care of his mate without her friend's help

TORI

He's tougher than he looks

Which is saying something, because he looks really damn tough

LOVE

If you want to leave, just leave, Sienna

ME

I should

TORI

But you won't

ME

Bye, ladies

Love sent me an eye-rolling emoji, and I turned my phone off.

And took another sip of water.

She was right, honestly. I needed to leave.

But I wouldn't. Or more accurately, I couldn't.

I didn't want to hurt their feelings. Or abandon them.

And I knew the alphas would start giving out my address if I didn't entertain the damn wolves they'd called in from all over the world. Taking a mate was the only real way to protect myself. The fact that I didn't *want* a mate didn't mean much to them, considering the danger I was in.

So, I just sipped my water.

"Is Bauther on your protective duty tonight?" one of the ladies next to me, Melissa, asked.

The other one, Belle, peered over her shoulder.

My gaze followed hers, and landed on Bauther, the beta of the pack. The beta was the alpha's right hand, and they both led the enforcers, who helped keep the pack safe.

Bauther was, admittedly, the most attractive werewolf I'd ever met. They were all tall and muscular, but he was stronger than most. With tan skin and long, dark blond hair he usually wore tied up in a bun, the man always caught my eye.

He was somehow both confident, but calm.

Strong, without being intimidating, too.

Most of the wolf guys I'd met had a rough sort of dominance, but Bauther could maintain control without barking orders. And that was kind of impressive.

"Yep. He's on duty eighty percent of the time," I explained. Madd was Love's alpha's nickname—his full name was Archer Madden.

"He doesn't look at you like a guard would," Belle remarked.

Yeah, I'd noticed.

My friends had too.

Love and Tori had been trying to convince me to let him pop my cherry for months, but I still hadn't talked to him for more than a few seconds at a time.

Honestly, Bauther was intimidating.

All that sex appeal was a *lot.*

Having a one-on-one conversation with a man that gorgeous still seemed like a risk.

Sleeping with him?

Wayyy riskier.

I always wore a ton of perfume to hide my scent, just to maintain my independence a little longer. Eventually, I was going to get stuck with some obnoxious wolf-man who would probably succeed at walking all over me.

Until then, I was satisfied with my virginity, and with ignoring Bauther's intense stare.

I took another sip of my water, looking pointedly away from him.

"You should ask him out," Belle said.

I ruffled my hair a bit, trying not to let myself get stressed. It was naturally honey-blonde, and I usually let it grow down to the middle of my back. I'd chopped it to my collarbone a while after moving to Wildwood, since it had been in terrible shape, so it looked decent.

Not great, but decent.

Still, I usually just put it up in a ponytail.

"Has he ever hit on you?" Melissa asked.

"No." If he had ever tried, I'd walked in the other direction so fast he didn't get the chance.

"Huh."

"Yep."

I took another sip of water.

Maybe pretending Tori was sick wasn't such a bad idea after all.

"He's probably waiting for you to make the first move, since you're a blood wolf and all. And the alphas trying to get you mated probably makes it a little taboo," Belle added.

"Ooh, taboo is sexy," Melissa said.

"I'm going to run to the bathroom." I set my glass down. They'd keep an eye on it. "Be right back."

They watched me cross the room, leaving my bag hanging off the back of the chair. As usual, I had on a pair of comfy leggings, and a sweater with a cat on it. And cat hair, which was an accessory I could never quite be free of.

My cat and I were sort of arch enemies. My wolf certainly hated her.

I locked the door to the ladies' bathroom behind me and spent a solid five minutes panic-scrolling on social media. I hoped it would reduce the uncertainty I'd started to feel about Bauther.

It didn't.

And it felt too weird to stay in the bathroom any longer.

So, when my five minutes was up, I flushed the toilet like I'd actually used it, then washed my hands for good measure. If someone was waiting out there, I didn't want them to realize I'd been hiding.

Was that weird?

It was probably weird.

I was feeling too panicky to care.

So I stepped out of the bathroom—and halted abruptly when I found a huge, beautiful man in front of me.

I was average height for a woman, around 5'5", but he still towered over me by an entire foot.

And holy shit, he was gorgeous.

He smelled just as good as he looked, too. My wolf lifted her head in the strange space where one of us remained while the other was in control, but she didn't say anything. Just studied him.

His eyes moved down my face slowly.

"Um, hi," I blurted, not sure what else to say to Bauther.

We hadn't had an actual conversation since I gave him a cookie a few months ago. That had been stupidly awkward. I'd dropped crumbs on my boobs, and he'd totally checked them out.

"Hey." Bauther's gaze lifted back to my eyes.

My face warmed. "Hi."

Shit, I'd already said that.

I started to take a step away, ready to make my escape, but he stopped me with a question.

"Can I buy you a drink?"

I glanced over at the ladies I'd left at my table.

They were both staring at us.

I couldn't exactly reject him while they were watching, could I?

I finally looked back at him. "Sure."

Wow, his eyes were pretty.

A shade of dark blue that I felt like I could fall into.

That was weird, though.

There would be no falling into anyone's eyes.

Especially not Bauther's.

He offered his elbow, and I took it. While I was reluctant to do so, I tried not to let it show.

When he gestured me toward a barstool, I sat down. It was sandwiched between his stool and the wall, which was either good or bad.

I wasn't sure which.

The bartender—Jerri, who I also knew from the pack—came over with a smile. Her gaze flicked between us, and her eyebrows lifted a bit. Her smile grew slightly. "What can I get you guys?"

"Coke would be good," I said.

I'd use the sugar and tiny bit of caffeine to propel me through what might be a very awkward conversation.

Bauther didn't look surprised at all by my order.

He *had* been following me for a while.

"Dr. Pepper for me," Bauther said.

I lifted my eyebrows.

He raised his at me when Jerri stepped away to grab her drink.

"You don't drink?" I asked him.

"Not when my date doesn't."

"Is this a date, then?" My question came out fast, and a bit alarmed.

I couldn't help it.

He was too beautiful.

"Yes."

The confidence in his answer caught me off guard too. "Why is it a date?"

Dammit, I needed to learn how to think before I spoke.

"You're gorgeous, and kind. Do I need another reason?"

I blinked at him.

What was I supposed to say to that?

"And the alphas invited someone you really won't like tonight. Oxford Retti," he added.

I blinked again. "Why won't I like him?"

"Ox is the alpha of the roughest pack in the country. He doesn't ask for permission."

And I could be a real doormat sometimes.

It was a problem.

I knew it was a problem.

I just hadn't figured out how to fix that about myself yet.

"Hopefully he's not my mate, then," I said with a sigh. "The other girls will probably point me out to him when he gets here."

"Not if you're with me."

"They can't be dissuaded. I've tried."

"They're enforcers. Madd's not here, so they answer to me. The guys he's inviting to town get more than enough of you as it is; you don't need to risk anything with Ox."

He caught me off guard with that, too, but I wasn't mentioning it.

I didn't talk about my issues with saying no. Especially not around tall, beautiful men.

Or *any* men.

Or any *women*, outside my two friends who were close enough to be considered sisters. Really, I didn't even like to talk about it with them.

"I didn't think you were interested in going out with me," I finally said. "Guess this makes more sense than the date thing anyway. Thanks, I think."

"Of course I'm interested in going out with you. Every unmated male in the pack is interested in going out with you, Sienna."

My face warmed.

That obviously wasn't true.

But I was almost vain enough to hope it was.

Almost.

Not quite, though.

"They all know I'm not looking for a mate."

"You make that clear with the lotion and perfume you wear." He waved a hand in front of his nose quickly, and I couldn't stop the laugh that escaped me.

"So this is a real date?"

"Of course it is. I couldn't resist any longer."

My face warmed further. "Well, you know how to flatter a woman."

"Not any woman. Just you." His knee brushed mine, and more warmth spread through my body.

It had to be a lie, but it made me feel good anyway.

Our attention lifted back to Jerri as she set the sodas down in front of us, along with a tray of fries.

"Some salt and grease to balance out the sugar," she said with a wink. "Enjoy."

We were both silent as she stepped away.

I grabbed a fry and took a big bite, just to give my mouth something to do other than telling Bauther how pretty he was.

"What's it like to be the beta?" I asked, when he sipped his drink rather than continuing the conversation. Despite his momentary silence, the *date* wasn't nearly as awkward as expected.

It wasn't awkward at all, actually.

It was kind of fun.

I liked flirting, even if I didn't do it much.

"A pain in my ass."

I laughed.

His lips curved upward slightly. "The female enforcers drive me crazy. They're always in everyone's business. They're the opposite of you and your friends."

"Our trauma taught us to deal with our own shit and keep our noses down." I took another fry. "I wish I had the guts to be as nosy as they are. It would be awesome to have access to all the juicy drama. I like to stay out of things, but I still want to know about them."

"You like drama, huh?"

"Oh, yes. I *live* for drama."

His lips curved upward, and he leaned toward me.

Something told me he had drama for me, so I leaned in too.

"Jerri's pregnant," he murmured. "Only a few weeks along, so they're not telling anyone yet."

My eyes widened. "How do you know this?"

"I'm the beta. I hear everything."

"Tell me more."

"Come home with me, and I will."

Ohh.

Wow.

That sly invitation was totally hot.

"I don't have sex on the first date," I warned.

I'd never even had a first date before. Or a second. Or *sex*.

"Neither do I."

"Good," I agreed. "You have to tell Belle and Melissa for me, and grab my bag, though."

His eyes gleamed. "No problem."

He set some cash on the bar, then strode over to the table where my friends sat. I looked pointedly at my drink, not sure I'd have the balls to leave if they looked disappointed or upset in any way.

Bauther was back a minute later, with my simple, fuzzy brown crossbody bag over his shoulder. Tori had bought it for me, and I was slightly obsessed with it. It kind of reminded me of my cat, although the reminder was usually unwanted considering how much she disliked me.

He offered me his hand. "Ready?"

Yes.

No?

I had no idea.

What did it take to be ready to go on a date with someone?

"Sure." I took his hand and flashed him a smile, like I had my crap together.

Which I didn't.

And never had.

But he didn't need to know that.

His lips brushed my knuckles—which made me warm even though I didn't question why his nostrils flared when he did —and let him lead me out of the bar.

Maybe a date would be fun.

SIENNA

THE DRIVE to his house was better than the time we'd spent in the bar.

He was much more relaxed, and I was too.

As much as I liked the other women in the pack, I needed a break from them.

"Do you have a middle name?" he asked. The topic was random, but I liked it.

"Yep. Most basic middle name there is. Sienna Ann. What about you?"

"No middle name. Usually go by my last name, as you know."

"I've never heard anyone call you by your first name," I agreed. "Except the humans I work with. They go on and on about you and Madd. Their voices take on this sultry tone every time they say your name. *Beckett Bauther*." I lowered my voice, trying to imitate their seductive voices.

He chuckled. "My parents call me Beckett. They're the only ones."

"They don't just call you Beck?"

"Nope."

"Hmm. Well, Beck fits you. I've never had a nickname before. Tori and Love have always told me I don't need one, because my name is sexy, which I think is total bullshit."

"Your name *is* sexy."

I rolled my eyes. "It's really not."

"I don't know why you'd think that."

Probably because I'd spent my childhood with parents who cared more about booze and drugs than they cared about me, and my teenage years as a living blood bag.

And because at twenty-four, I still hadn't ever had sex.

As much as I wanted to try it, I couldn't bring myself to trust anyone enough to take the risk.

I changed the subject. "Which part of the neighborhood is your house in?"

He eyed me, obviously noticing my subject change, but didn't call me out on it. "The opposite side of yours."

He knew where I lived.

Considering he'd been following me for ages, that was obvious.

"So you're in the front corner?"

"Yep."

"Okay. Are you going to tell me more drama now?"

He flashed me an amused look. "You're an addict."

"Oh, I know." I leaned toward him. "Come on, Beck."

"Alright." He considered it, his gaze flicking to me in the mirror. "The Finches are moving out of the pack's neighborhood. They want to fix up an old house in the forest and join Ronin's pack. Tia is going to ask Tori sometime this week. We warned them they might get turned down, but I don't think Vex will be against letting his pack grow a little. The entire pack doesn't have to be government even though it is right now."

"Ooh, scandalous. Tori will be thrilled." The Wildwood Pack had been growing madly, and was in the process of expanding the neighborhood because of it.

I didn't blame the Finches for wanting to get out before it exploded even more.

"They're taking some heat from a few of their closest friends," he added.

I tsked my tongue. "How dare they be independent."

He chuckled. "That seems to be the attitude."

"How do you feel about them moving out?"

He lifted a shoulder. "It's their life. I'll never leave, but I can see why some people would."

"I feel the same. Well, not about never leaving. I haven't decided about that. But about it being their life."

"Where would you go if you left?" There was something between curiosity and caution in his gaze when it flicked to me.

"I don't know. Scale Ridge is pretty, and it would be cool to see the dragons flying overhead every now and then."

"Scale Ridge is run by three demon brothers, and a vampire clan that only lives by the laws that won't get them killed by the demons."

I grimaced. "Not Scale Ridge, then. Maybe Wolfcrest."

"There are a handful of powerful fae that control Wolfcrest. They ran out the wolves that founded it long before the war between humans and supernaturals."

The war had ended a century earlier, and supernaturals had become a normal part of life for humans. We were like low-level celebrities—some people were obsessed with the idea of us, but others didn't give a shit.

My grimace deepened. "Guess I'm staying."

I rolled my window down and took in a deep breath of the clean, fresh air.

If I was going to be stuck somewhere, Wildwood was far from the worst option. It was peaceful and calm, the city nestled in the forest so completely that it felt much smaller than it was. Maybe some supernaturals would like a big-city feel, but I wasn't one of them.

Wind whipped through my hair, and my lips curved upward as we passed massive, old trees.

I felt safe in the forest.

Free, too.

My wolf stretched languidly. *"I like Wildwood,"* she murmured into my mind.

"So do I," I admitted.

"I like Bauther, too."

I didn't want to tell her I felt the same way. *"We're not looking for a mate."*

"Mating could be dangerous."

But her interest in the man beside me was so evident, I wasn't sure I believed her.

There was too much shit in my past to let myself consider that, though.

"He would be more aggressive if we were fated mates, don't you think?" I asked her. *"There's no way Vex or Madd would've followed Tori or Love around for so long if there was a bond between them. Werewolf guys are desperate for mates."*

"I don't think any male wolf would be as patient as him if he knew we were his mate. But we also haven't given a potential mate any reason to be aggressive yet."

"How would we do that?"

"Flirting with another man. Stripping in public."

"Even if by some chance we were mated, he has no way to know while I cover my scent," I finally said. *"You know I'm obsessive about hiding it. I put lotion or deodorant everywhere, and perfume on top of it."*

"I know. We should be safe from any potential bond. Plenty of werewolves sleep around until they meet their mate—he may just want some physical contact and think you're pretty."

My face warmed at the idea.

I liked it, a lot.

How good he smelled to me had to be a coincidence.

"Let's go with that option," I said. *"He might have been lying about not having sex on the first date."*

"There's plenty of fun to be had before you get to sex, right?"

My face flushed. *"Supposedly."*

My wolf chuffed, her version of laughter, and curled back up comfortably as Bauther pulled into the garage of his house.

It was in the furthest corner of the street closest to the neighborhood's entrance, big but not massive, and surrounded by even more trees than most of the homes.

"You like your privacy," I remarked, as he parked and shut off the engine.

"I do." He stepped out and made it around the truck quickly enough to open my door for me while I was still pulling my bag over my shoulder. When he offered his hand, I took it. My lips curved upward automatically as he helped me down.

He didn't release my hand as he led me inside the house behind him. My gaze moved over the interior—the walls were light and floors were dark, with everything looking sort of rustic and rugged.

It felt comfortable, and natural.

"Your home is beautiful, Beck."

"Thank you." He squeezed my hand lightly, and I bit my lip to stop myself from smiling again.

I needed to get my emotions back under control. I was enjoying our date way too much.

"Did you have dinner yet?" he asked.

"Yes, before we went out. The bar's fries are good, but they're about the only edible thing they sell."

He chuckled, leading me to the couch. "I agree."

My body warmed a bit more. I was feeling sort of... well, horny.

I'd never felt horny because of someone before.

I liked it, though.

Bauther sat first, leaving me to decide how much distance I put between us.

I gave in to my horniness and sat down close to him, turning so the top of my knee rested on his thigh. His hand landed on my leg immediately, and my body warmed further.

"So do you have more drama for me?" I teased.

"Always." He squeezed my leg, and I felt myself getting damp between my thighs.

"Anne Singer and Gordon Long have hated each other for years."

"Everyone knows that. He drives her insane."

"And she makes him crazy. But a few weeks ago, a mate bond bloomed between them."

My eyes nearly bulged out of my head. "No way."

"Yep. They've been fighting it, but the enforcers are all putting bets on how long they'll make it before they give in."

"Holy shit. How do you even fight a mate bond?" I'd seen Love and Tori try, but they had been really bad at avoiding their men. And the guys were so dominant that they didn't let the girls get away with it for long.

"They're refusing to see each other. When their wolves take over and run together, they go their separate ways as soon as they can shift back."

"Wow. Could they go on like that forever?"

"Assuming they seal the bond and don't let themselves start to like each other, yes. Without sealing it, the wolves will take over more and more, becoming much more dominant over their humans until they have no choice but to make it permanent."

As bad as sealing the bond and living apart sounded, it was a better option than moving in together if they didn't like each other.

I'd seen first-hand how bad relationships could be, so I for one wasn't interested in the slightest.

"Wow. That's insane."

"Lex and Arnold did the same thing for a while, before they eventually gave in to the bond," he said. "It's more common than some werewolves realize."

"I definitely didn't realize."

He squeezed my knee.

I wanted more.

"Do you want to watch a movie?" The words spilled from my lips quickly.

A movie seemed like my best bet of snuggling up with him, and maybe getting to the next level.

"Sure." His gaze didn't leave me for a moment. "Unless you want to do something else."

"Like..."

"Like kiss me."

Ohhh.

"What happened to no sex on the first date?" My voice was playful, though I was already slipping my shoes off and dropping my bag on the couch.

"There's plenty to do before we get to sex."

His words echoed my wolf's.

"Sounds like fun." I put a leg over his lap, and his hands found the backs of my thighs, pulling me closer.

His chest rumbled as I sat down over his erection. He was hard against my center—and felt unbelievably good. My leggings and his jeans separated us, but I didn't give a damn about that.

His hand slid around the back of my head, cupping my face before he pulled me closer.

My lips met his softly, and I was surprised by the sensations.

Soft.

Warm.

Light.

"Do you do this often?" I asked, my voice breathless as I pulled back.

"No." His grip tightened on the backs of my thighs. "Do you?"

"Never."

His eyes grew hot.

His chest rumbled with satisfaction.

And his lips met mine again.

This time, his tongue met the seam of my lips, and I opened for him.

His chest rumbled again, louder, as our tongues collided.

Holy hell, he tasted incredible.

I wanted more of him.

I *needed* more of him.

My wolf whispered something, but I didn't hear it.

My tongue moved with his, hot and desperate.

And despite the desperation, it was *fun*. Way more fun than I would've expected.

We kissed for ages, the kiss hot and heady.

Until his hand on the back of my thigh slid up to my ass, and I arched slightly.

The motion rocked me against his erection—and I loved that.

I *needed* that.

I felt myself rumbling a little too, almost like I was purring at the sensation.

Our mouths moved together, our tongues dancing and warring.

Bauther used his grip on my ass to rock me against him.

I paused and sucked in a breath, but he didn't stop kissing me.

His tongue stroked mine, confident and sure.

I moved my hips—and gasped at the feel of it.

Of him.

I wanted his clothes gone.

Mine, too.

I managed to get his shirt off of him before his lips and tongue found my throat. He kissed, licked, and sucked the sensitive skin as I moved again.

He moved me, too.

Again, and again.

Need and pleasure tensed in my lower belly until I finally lost control.

I cried out desperately as pleasure rolled through me, all the way down to my toes. My breaths were uneven as I tried to recover, but his hand was still on my ass, and I still wanted more.

"You're fucking gorgeous," he growled.

I arched against him again, and he slid his hand up the curve of my waist.

"Let me touch you," he said.

"You can do whatever the hell you want to me, if it feels that good."

His fingers hooked under my sweater, pulling it up over my head.

My stomach tensed as he undid my nude, lace bra—and I gasped as his rough hands slid over my breasts a moment later.

He squeezed and kneaded, dragging his thumbs over my nipples.

My hips moved as he touched me.

"You're so damn soft." He increased the pressure to my nipples, and I moaned. "Bet you'll taste good, too."

My entire body clenched at the thought.

His tongue was dragging over one of my nipples a moment later.

I cried out, hips jerking desperately. The pressure on my clit through our clothes still felt good, but it wasn't enough. I wanted his jeans gone.

He sucked lightly, and I swear, my brain short-circuited.

"Even better than I thought." His voice was low, almost feral.

My head tipped back.

Desperate noises I hadn't realized I was capable of making filled the air as he played with my nipples with his hands, tongue, and teeth.

And despite his jeans—which I'd come to despise—the pressure of him and the way he made love to my breasts was too much.

My cries flooded the room as I bucked and rocked, unraveling against him again.

"Holy shit," I moaned, his tongue still dragging over one of my nipples and his thumb slowly teasing the other.

"Next time, you climax on my tongue."

"*Yes.*" The word was desperate.

Hot.

So insanely needy.

I had to have more.

His mouth and hands left my breasts, moving slowly down my abdomen as he lowered me to the rug on the floor.

If not for the orgasms that had relaxed me, I might've been self-conscious about being naked in front of him.

I might've been worried he wouldn't like the way I looked.

But he'd made it really damn clear that he loved my body.

And as he stripped my leggings off, his chest was rumbling again. The sound of his satisfaction made me even hotter. "You wear thongs?"

"Basically required with leggings," I managed to say.

His hands slid up my bare thighs, parting my legs wider so he could see more of me, covered only by a thin strip of nude lace that matched my bra.

My breaths came out rapidly, my eyes fixed on his big hands as they slid over my skin.

A cry escaped me when I watched his thumb slide over my clit once, and again, over the top of my panties. When he slowly began dragging them down my thighs, my gaze remained fixed on the hand he left at my core, still working me.

"You like watching me touch you, Si?" I loved the way he shortened my name like I'd shortened his.

"So much," I managed.

He left his thumb on my clit as he grabbed a pillow off the couch with his free hand, then tucked it behind my head. "Then watch me taste you."

My breathing grew shallow as he lowered himself between my thighs.

And slowly dragged his tongue over my clit.

A louder, more desperate cry escaped me.

My hips bucked as he licked me again.

My body trembled.

The sounds of my pleasure filled the air when he dragged his teeth over my clit, bringing me release like I'd never experienced it before.

"Fucking hell," I moaned, as I came down from the high. "I had no idea I could feel like that."

His chest rumbled in satisfaction. "Keep your eyes on me. You can give me another climax."

I groaned, but didn't dare look away.

It took longer the next time—but neither of us gave a damn about the time.

He made me cry out again.

And again.

My body felt like a damn noodle when he finally dragged his mouth down my inner thigh, sucking lightly before he pulled his lips away. "You're a fucking dream, Sienna."

He was the dream, not me.

But I wasn't about to tell him that.

Not when it might stop him from wanting a redo of the night we'd shared.

Or even *more*.

He grabbed my leggings off the floor and helped me pull them up my shaking legs. I was still drenched between my thighs, thanks to both his mouth and my body's reaction to it, but I didn't ask him for a towel.

I knew werewolves enough to know he'd like the thought of leaving his mark on me like that, even though we weren't mates.

Werewolves were possessive as hell, after all.

Myself included, though I'd never had a reason to be possessive of anyone other than my best friends.

He pulled my sweater over my head without my bra, but I was too blissed-out to even notice.

"I should probably go," I said, my voice soft.

"Let me get you a plate of food to take home."

He wanted to take care of me.

That was really, really sweet.

But way too mate-like. I couldn't let him think I was interested in a relationship. He had a fated mate out there somewhere—and I did too. Neither of us would be able to stay together if we met our mate.

And even if we didn't, I wasn't interested in a mate bond.

So as much as I hated saying no, I had to turn him down.

"I've got leftovers," I murmured. "Thank you, though."

He nodded a bit stiffly, but grabbed my shoes off the floor and my bag off the couch for me. The bag went over his shoulder, and the shoes in his hand.

His free hand found my lower back and led me toward the door.

The simple, gentle touch made me ache to ask if I could stay the night. Or if he wanted to come home with me.

But that was a bad idea.

A terrible idea.

So I didn't.

I did, however, lean against him as he walked me home.

And kiss him on my doorstep. His mouth tasted like me, and that made my toes curl.

When he released my mouth, he dragged his thumb over my bottom lip. It felt a little swollen.

His voice was low and gravelly. "What are you doing tomorrow?"

"Working," I whispered.

"Can I take you to dinner?"

He knew where I worked, and when I got off.

"That depends," I finally said. "Do you have sex on the second date?"

"With you, I do."

My lips curved upward. "Will it be as good as tonight?"

"It'll be *better*, Sienna."

My lower belly tightened. "Pick me up at five."

His chest rumbled. "Four."

My smile widened. "Three-thirty."

He kissed me again, harder. His tongue tangled with mine, and the taste of my pleasure made me so damn excited for the next day. "I'll see you then. Get some sleep, Si."

"You too."

He gave me one last, light kiss, handed me my purse and shoes, and finally stepped back.

I fiddled with the zipper on my bag before I managed to get my keys out. My hand was still a little unsteady as I unlocked the door, but I got it open.

He was still waiting on the porch to make sure I made it safely inside, when I stepped in.

I turned, my eyes meeting his. "Thanks, Beck. I had fun."

"So did I. Sleep well."

"You too."

I finally, reluctantly, closed the door between us.

My cat greeted me with an annoyed hiss, and for once, it didn't make me feel like shit.

I'd had the best night of my life.

three

BAUTHER

MY HAND WORKED MY COCK, the other spread on the shower wall.

Sienna's cries were in my ears.

Her taste was on my tongue.

Her scent was in my lungs.

I'd jerked off three times in the hours since I'd left her, but it wasn't enough.

It would never fucking be enough.

My wolf urged me to go to her.

To be at her side.

But if I pushed her too hard, too quickly, she'd run. Or at the very least, push me away. And if not push me away, resent me for pressuring her the way the alpha and the pack's females did.

My mate didn't know how to tell people no.

I'd tried like hell not to let myself take advantage of that. She needed to know she was safe with me, no matter what.

My balls tightened, and I swore as I found my release again.

It barely took the edge off my need for her.

If I was with her, it would've been different.

But I had to give her that damn space. She needed time to realize for herself what we were—and I couldn't push her into it.

No matter how badly I wanted to.

Patience.

I had to have patience.

There was a knock at my door.

I ignored it.

When it sounded again, it was more impatient.

I ignored it again.

There was a moment's pause before I heard it open.

"What the fuck happened last night?" Madd growled from the front room.

I cursed under my breath, but turned the shower off and grabbed a towel. My jeans from the night before went back on.

They smelled like my mate.

I tucked the panties I'd stolen from her into my pocket.

Hopefully, they would ground me.

I'd kept her bra too—but it was already tucked beneath the blankets of my bed. It would make the mattress smell like her, which might help me sleep.

I didn't bother with a shirt, drying my hair with a towel as I strode out to the kitchen. Madd was leaning against the cabinets, his arms folded.

"Lovene woke me up in the middle of the night because her friend was missing. When I called around, I found out she was with *you*." His eyes narrowed at me. "You took her out of the bar before she met Ox. You know we thought he would be the one."

"And you know I said he was too rough for her."

"You don't make decisions for her, Bauther. I'm her alpha."

"And I'm her mate."

His eyes narrowed further.

I let out a steadying breath, then tossed my towel on the counter, crossed the kitchen, and opened the fridge.

Hopefully, I'd find something that would ease my need to be beside her.

I didn't.

"Since when?" Madd demanded.

"I've suspected for months, but knew she wouldn't react well to an alpha-style mate abduction."

"Suspecting isn't enough, Bauther."

"Last night, she washed her hands, and gave me the chance to smell them. Her scent was faint, but it was there. When I brought her home, my theory was confirmed, and there's no longer any doubt."

That was all the information he was getting.

He gave an annoyed growl. "I've been trying to find her mate for months, and you've been hiding this from me. While she's been hiding from you."

"Of course she has. Her life was hell before she came to Wildwood."

He made a reluctant noise of agreement.

While we both knew how blood wolves were created, he was the only one who had heard the story directly from one of them.

"Why aren't you with her now, then? You told her she's yours, didn't you?" Madd asked.

"No."

He scoffed.

I shut the fridge, turning toward him. "Sienna isn't Love. She doesn't show it often, but she's scared. I have to let her realize on her own that we're mates. If I tell her, she'll shut me down."

"Secrets are the wrong way to start a relationship," Madd warned. "The woman will castrate you when she realizes you didn't tell her."

"Or she'll be too attached to me to push me away for long," I countered.

"You're a damn moron, Bauther."

"I said the same thing when you threw your mate in prison."

The judgment on his face eased. "That was a misunderstanding."

"And this is my best attempt at making her comfortable."

His judgment eased further. "I want it in the records that I disagreed with this."

"Fine. Make sure Love doesn't tell her anything."

He grunted. "I don't control my female."

I narrowed my eyes at him. "Then don't tell her what you know."

"Fine. If I tell her, I'll make sure she knows she has to keep the secret."

"Good."

Madd crossed the space between us and slapped me on the back. "I'm happy for you, man."

"Thanks."

With that, he strode out of the kitchen. As he walked out through the front door, he called out, "Good luck. You might want to ask Belle to keep her mouth shut if you're really wanting it quiet. The women's group chats were pretty active last night."

Shit.

He shut the door behind himself, but I had it open again and was jogging down the street in the opposite direction thirty seconds later.

My fist pounded on the door to Belle's house. We weren't close, but we'd known each other since we were pups, and she was one of my enforcers.

I waited impatiently, but she finally pulled it open, rubbing her eyes. She was still in her pajamas, but we were close enough that neither of us gave a damn. "What the hell, Bauther? It's not even seven yet."

"What did you say in the women's group chats?" I growled.

She blinked.

I held my hand out. "Give me your phone."

She sighed, but handed it over.

She gave me the passcode and watched as I pulled up the *Wildwood Bitches* group chat. I neither came up with the name nor supported it, though it made me snort the first time I heard about it. It was the pack women's favorite way of keeping in contact.

I scrolled up until I found a picture Belle had sent of me leading Sienna away from the bar.

Both of us were smiling.

I grimaced, scrolling through the messages.

WENDY

OMG

JULIE

They're so cute together!

HOPE

I LOVE IT

SABRINA

Is this a mate thing or a sex thing?

CASSIE

Someone needs to find out pronto

JOY

Does Bauther sleep around? I need answers!

AMBER

OBSESSED

HALEY

I tried to hit on him once and he didn't go for it.

ASHLEY

That doesn't mean he doesn't sleep around

BELLE

He doesn't usually hook up with packmates, but I don't know if it's a mate thing

KAYBREE

I HOPE THEY'RE MATES

EMMEE

How adorable would that be?!

TAYLOR

Sienna doesn't want a mate though

ZOEY

Anyone with eyes would want a mate if it was Bauther

ANNIE

That man is delicious

HANNAH

And doesn't he have like four master's degrees?

CHLOE

He does.

BECCA

Yummm.

KYLEE

I want a Bauther.

BELLE

Someone needs to ask Tori and Love about this

ASHLEY

Do they know anything?

LOVE

No, they don't

TORI

We're trying to find out. She's not answering her phone.

SABRINA

I wouldn't answer my phone if I was having
dirty, dirty sex with that gorgeous man
either

BELLE

No one with a brain cell would

I scrolled through more of the messages, looking for any response from Sienna or her best friends. None of them replied to the chat again, though the women went on and on about me.

I checked the female enforcers group, and saw more of the same shit.

Nothing from Sienna, or her friends.

That was a relief, at least.

I handed Belle her phone back, and she had an expectant expression on her face. Since she'd given me access to a conversation I shouldn't have been able to read, I knew I was obligated to tell her what was going on.

"I've suspected Sienna is my mate since she got to town. There was a pull to her—it was magnetic. I didn't get a whiff of her scent to prove it until last night."

Belle's eyes lit up. "She's really yours?"

I dipped my head. "But she doesn't want a mate."

Though her eyes were still bright, she frowned. "What did she say when you told her, then?"

"I didn't tell her. I'm just going to be her friend for now."

Her gaze grew skeptical. "It was more than friendly at the bar last night, and no one missed the way she went home with you."

"Boyfriend, then. Eventually, she'll realize what I am to her. I'm hoping she'll be too attached to me to run when she finds out."

Belle grimaced. "That is a *terrible* idea."

"What's the alternative? I tell her, and watch her walk away? Or pressure her into agreeing to seal the bond?"

Her forehead wrinkled further. "It's a difficult situation."

"I know."

"I still think your plan is shitty," she finally said.

"It is," I agreed. "But better than the alternatives. She needs the freedom to figure it out herself."

Belle sighed. "I guess. She's going to be pissed when she finds out the truth, though."

"Undoubtedly."

She tucked her hair behind her ear. "I've got to go, but I assume you're here to tell me to keep my mouth shut?"

"Yep." I nodded in confirmation.

"No one will hear any more news about you two from me. I have to participate in the group conversations from time to time though, or they'll get suspicious."

"That's fine. Just don't tell them anything. And get them to stop sending pictures of us."

She agreed, and I headed back home.

Now I just had to survive eight and a half hours without going to my mate.

SIENNA

I CHATTED with the other girls working the same way I usually did. Every time I made eye contact with Tori, she grinned and shook her head at me.

She was proud of me for having the courage to say yes when Bauther asked me out, and for sleeping with him, but she warned me to be careful not to get attached. Being with him more than once was risky, considering we both had mates out there somewhere.

But still, all was well.

Life was good.

Minus the *Wildwood Bitches* group chat, of course.

I kind of wanted to murder all of the *bitches*.

But life was still good.

Everything was fine.

I was great.

I usually had that group chat muted so my phone didn't go off all day, but after I'd read the messages going on and on about how sexy Beck was, I'd turned the notifications on.

If they were talking about him, I wanted to know.

My phone buzzed on the table, where I'd left it while I frosted skeleton-shaped sugar cookies. Of all the bakers, I was the best at decorating cookies, so I'd been having a blast making fun designs for Halloween since it was approaching.

When I saw the text on the screen, I scowled.

> **EMMEE**
>
> Did anyone get any news about Sienna and Bauther?
>
> **ASHLEY**
>
> No. I keep checking, hoping he's still on the market. I've had a fantasy that I wake up one morning and find out I'm fated to that man for years.
>
> **HALEY**
>
> lol
>
> **AMBER**
>
> Same
>
> **HANNAH**
>
> No news is probably good news. I bet they're just having some fun.

My scowl became a glare.

We *were* just having some fun.

But that didn't mean I wanted any other women thinking about Beck.

Or sleeping with him.

Holy hell, what if he'd had sex with some of them?

Or what if he was sleeping with one of them, *and* with me?

My brain was going to short-circuit again.

I dropped the half-frosted skeleton and grabbed my phone.

"I'm going on break," I told the other girls.

If they said anything in response, I didn't hear it.

I tossed my gloves in the trash bin when I reached our tiny break room, and collapsed in a chair. While instinct screamed at me not to, I pulled up Beck's number and sent a quick message.

ME

Are you sleeping with anyone else in the pack?

He didn't make me wait, his text coming through almost instantly.

BAUTHER

No

The tension in my shoulders eased slightly.

Except I had to try to get out of the conversation without explaining my random question.

Yikes.

ME

K

BAUTHER

K?

ME

K

BAUTHER

What do you mean, k?

ME

OK

BAUTHER

But why did you ask?

I started typing an answer, but couldn't come up with anything that didn't make me sound slightly insane. So, I finally just exited the text thread.

Of course, my phone rang almost as soon as I did so.

My stomach clenched, but I had to answer. He knew I was on my phone.

"Hello?" I said, trying to sound like my usual self.

"Hey." His voice made goosebumps break out on my arms.

And it brought my mind back to the night before.

My face flushed, and I couldn't help but remember him telling me how good I tasted.

"Why did you ask if I was sleeping with anyone else in the pack?" His question was direct.

Too direct to dance around it.

I grimaced. "There's been a lot of messages about you in the women's group chat after last night. I started thinking about it and just got stuck in my head I guess. When I tried to explain myself, I realized how ridiculous I sounded."

"Werewolves are possessive, Sienna. That's nature. It's not ridiculous. If I found out you were fucking another guy in the pack after last night, I would probably kill the bastard."

My shoulders eased. "I *shouldn't* be possessive, though. We didn't talk about being exclusive or anything."

"We made plans for tonight. I was going to make plans for tomorrow after tonight, too, so it's a hell of a lot more than one night. I'm yours for the foreseeable future, alright? And if we're sleeping together, it's exclusive."

His words relaxed me, though my face was still warm. "Alright."

"Ignore what the women in the pack say. They can talk as much shit as they want."

"They're not talking shit. They're... I don't know. In *love* with you."

He chuckled. "They barely know me, Sienna. I'm just the beta to them. I've never had sex with someone in the pack before you. Remember that when they get too loud."

I nodded, though he couldn't see me. "Alright."

"I'll see you at 3:30?" he asked.

"Yep. 3:30." I ran my fingers through my tangled ponytail. I'd slept in too late to fix it, so it didn't look great.

"Unless… have you had lunch yet?"

I was out of it after not sleeping much, so I had to glance at the clock. "No. Not for another hour."

"I can bring you something to eat, if you don't have plans with your friends."

My face heated further.

I didn't have plans, but…

Well, if I accepted, it would bring us closer together. And I didn't want a mate, or a committed relationship.

But he *wasn't* my mate.

And we couldn't commit to each other, given that we weren't mates.

So…

"Lunch would be nice."

"I'll pick something up on the way."

"Thank you." I bit my lip. "I need to get back to work."

"Alright. I'll see you soon."

"Bye." I hung up, biting my lip harder as I stared at my phone.

Tori crossed the small room and sat down in the chair beside mine, leaning back and studying me. She was tall, with strawberry-blonde hair cut in a pixie, and pale skin.

"Stop judging me," I said, my face still warm.

"I'm not judging you."

"You totally are."

Her lips curved upward. "You look happy, Sienna. Why would I judge you for that?"

"You think it's dangerous to sleep with someone who isn't my mate," I countered. "You think I could get attached. Or he could get attached. Or it could break my heart when he finds his mate. Or—"

"I don't think any of those things, but it seems like you do."

I heaved a sigh. "I don't know what I think anymore. I just know I don't want a mate. It's too risky."

Tori nodded. "I get it."

She was mated, but she'd been against it for ages too. She was the one who taught me how to put on enough perfume and lotion to hide my scent.

"And if I can't have a mate, why not have fun with Bauther right now, you know? He likes me, and I like him."

"And he has four masters' degrees, apparently."

I smiled.

"Just don't let yourself get too attached to him, and everything will be fine."

She was right.

I was shitty at not getting attached, though.

I'd just have to figure it out.

. . .

BAUTHER SHOWED up with lunch a few minutes early. I met him at the back door of the bakery, and couldn't help the thrill that rolled through me when I saw him.

"Hey," I said, not bothering to fight my smile.

"Hey. You look good." He tugged lightly on my ponytail, and I made a face.

"Didn't have much time this morning."

"I figured. Your hair is even prettier when I know it smells like me."

I laughed and pushed him lightly. He took a staggered step back, making me snort. The man was so solid, there was no way I'd actually moved him.

Stepping back up to my side, he laced his fingers through mine.

My chest warmed.

"Are you okay with eating in my truck? People will stare at us and take pictures if we eat inside." He gestured to the bakery—which was also a coffee shop that sold candy. Long story, but it was called *Coffee & Toffee & Cake*.

Bauther and Madd were both pretty well known by the humans, especially the ones in the city. They'd been leading the Wildwood pack for ages, and there were more than a few social-media-stalker pages about both of them.

"Definitely."

He opened the passenger door, and held my hand to help me inside.

Inside his truck, I found takeout boxes of Chinese food.

Yumm.

"Pick whichever you want," Beck said, his fingers ruffling my hair lightly. I made a face at him for playing with the strands, and he tugged in response.

We both opened our boxes and took bites.

"Okay, this is incredible," I said around my mouthful of food. It sounded more like, "Ohey, iss iss irrerible."

His hand landed on my thigh, and squeezed lightly.

I took another bite to stop myself from doing something crazy, like climbing on top of him and drinking his blood.

At the passing thought, my fangs itched and started to descend.

I shoved another bite in my mouth.

Friends with benefits.

That's all we were.

Friends with benefits.

"How's your day going?" he asked, distracting me from my desire to jump his bones.

I launched into a description of the newest cookies I was frosting (I was the shop's cookie decorator, though I did other stuff too). He asked questions, and kept me talking.

The conversation flowed naturally. By the time my alarm went off to remind me I needed to go back to work, I could hardly believe how fast it had gone by.

BAUTHER TEXTED ME AT THREE, while I was showering. I poked my head out of the shower to read the text, and couldn't help the thrill that raced down my spine.

> **BAUTHER**
> How do you feel about letting me cook for you tonight?

> **ME**
> Sounds perfect, see you soon <3

He liked the message, and I wiped the wet screen of my phone on my towel before dropping it and returning to my shower.

Soon enough, I was drying off and stepping out. As I reached for my bottle of lotion, it occurred to me that I might not need it.

After a moment of hesitation, I picked my phone up and texted my best friends again.

> **ME**
> Someone would know whether or not they were your fated mate after kissing you, right?

> **LOVE**
> Yes. Can't exactly hide your scent in your mouth.

TORI

Strong mouthwash and gum might do the job

But if you weren't chewing it last night, it's too late

ME

Then he's definitely not my mate, right?

TORI

If he let you walk away from him in the middle of the night, it seems highly unlikely

Unless he smells really good

Does he smell really good?

ME

Yes

TORI

Good enough that you have a hard time not biting him?

ME

...no?

TORI

You're probably safe then

ME

Probably?

LOVE

Have you tried asking him?

No male werewolf would lie to his mate if she questioned him directly. I don't think the wolf would allow it

ME

I don't want to ask him

> That would make things awkward

LOVE

Seems like a basic question before
jumping into relationship of casual sex.
Just go with a relaxed, "Hey, before we go
any further, you aren't thinking of me as
your mate, right?"

TORI

And if he says yes, leave

> ME

> He won't say yes. We're not mates!

TORI

If you're sure of that, there's no point in
wondering, is there?

I sighed, and didn't answer the message.

I was sure.

Fairly sure.

Pretty sure.

Sure-ish, at least.

And I didn't know if I was willing to risk letting him walk away. Not after how much fun I'd had the night before, and during lunch. We hadn't even done anything sexual when we shared a meal, and it had still been fun. It seemed like he just wanted to be my friend.

TORI

If it makes you feel any better, I can't see you mating with a beta. They're still pretty damn dominant. I think you need someone nicer

Bauther was nice, though.

Nice enough to intervene before I got stuck having a conversation with someone named Ox, who was apparently very forward and not great at taking no for an answer.

LOVE

But fate doesn't make sense sometimes. Can't count on it to be logical

TORI

Um, what? You were vocally against her and Bauther as anything more than sex buddies

ME

Why were either of you talking about me and Bauther?

TORI

That is not the point, Sienna

ME

I think it is

LOVE

Madd just got home, GTG. Good luck!

TORI

Okay, that was suspicious

I rubbed my temple, my stress so thick that I didn't know what I was going to do.

Ask him if he was my mate?

Go with my gut that he wasn't?

Something else altogether?

ME

I have to get ready for my date

TORI

Alright, I'll snoop a bit to see if I can figure out why Love's being weird.

Have fun! Don't overthink anything!

I groaned, dropping my phone on the countertop and ducking into my bedroom.

Most of the time I'd had to get ready was gone, so I pulled on a pair of panties and a bra. All of my underwear were soft lace, in varying neutral shades. I didn't really buy bright colors. They just didn't fit my personality. And my average-sized boobs were obnoxious enough in a bralette that I didn't dare buy a real, padded bra.

My leggings and a sweater followed. Neither of them were fancy. I didn't *own* anything fancy. I wasn't comfortable dressing that way, so even if I'd had fancy things, I probably wouldn't have worn them.

After I tugged a brush through my hair and swept some mascara on my lashes, I heard a knock.

Letting out a long breath, I made my way to the front door.

My cat hissed at me as I passed, and I winced.

She really hated me.

"We should find her a new home," my wolf grumbled, in response to the hiss.

"She's safe and happy here."

She hissed again.

"Safe, at least," I finally said.

My wolf grumbled, but didn't argue.

I tugged the door open, and my shoulders relaxed at the sight of the man on my porch.

Tall, tan, and gigantic.

His hair was tied up, showing the chiseled lines of his cheekbones.

And his lips curved upward when he saw me. His nostrils flared, and they flickered to another color for a second, as if his wolf had very nearly taken control. "You look good with your hair down."

My face warmed. "You probably do too."

I wasn't smooth.

Not smooth at all.

He grinned, though, lighting up his eyes and making my stomach clench. "You ready?"

"Yes." My cat hissed behind me, and I grimaced. "Maybe not. One second."

five

SIENNA

HE PEERED into the house as I stepped back, leaving the door open.

If I gave her a treat before I left, she wouldn't attack me when I got home.

"My cat is a dictator," I called over my shoulder, as I stepped into the pantry. "She calls the shots and she knows it."

He chuckled. "Can I meet her?"

"If you're okay with getting scratched, go ahead."

He stepped into the house and shut the front door.

"What's her name?" he asked.

"Sprinkles. I didn't name her, she's a rescue," I explained. "Although *terrorist* might fit better... What the hell?"

I stared at Bauther.

He was on his knees next to Sprinkles' climbing tower, and he had his hands on her fur.

Petting her.

He was *petting* her.

And she wasn't attacking him!

"You're a cat whisperer," I said, shock in my voice.

He laughed. "I don't think I've ever even touched a cat before, Si."

The nickname made me warm. "Well you're a Sprinkles whisperer, at least. She hates everyone. Especially me."

"I can't imagine anyone hating you."

"Well Sprinkles can't imagine anyone *liking* me."

He grinned.

I handed him the treat. "Here. Give this to her so she doesn't attack me when I get home."

"She's calm now. You do it." The look he flashed me wasn't a challenge, but it was almost one.

I didn't want to say no.

I didn't even want to argue.

Not because I wanted to make him happy. I wasn't really sure why, but making him happy didn't sound right.

I sat down next to him and handed her the treat.

She stole it from me more gently than she usually did.

That was a nice change.

I liked feeding her when it didn't involve nearly losing my fingers.

"Why did you get a cat in the first place?" he asked.

"I don't know. I was lonely, I guess. Tori was falling for Vex, and Love was talking about taking baths with Madd, and I just... A cat seemed like a safe option. A mate, not so much."

Bauther nodded, but didn't say anything else.

I remembered Love telling me to just come out and ask him if we were mates, but I knew that could ruin what we had going on.

And I liked what we had.

So, I didn't ask.

It still seemed unnecessary, too.

He would've told me if I was his mate. Wouldn't he?

"Ready?" I asked him.

"Sure." He stood up—scooping Sprinkles up with him.

She hissed, but it was half-hearted. And she didn't even scratch him.

"She's seriously in love with you," I complained. "You're not bringing her with us, are you? She'll freak out."

"Of course I am. Maybe she just doesn't like your house. Territory is a big thing for cats, isn't it?"

"I don't know. Maybe."

"It's important for wolves, so why not? Maybe my place will calm her down more."

The logic didn't seem sound, but I didn't give a damn about the logic.

As long as Sprinkles didn't intervene during the sexy times, she could come along.

If she did, my wolf just might eat her.

"It's worth a try," I agreed.

So, he carried her out of the house.

And all three of us made our way down the street. When he captured my hand, sliding his fingers between mine, it made me warm.

And happy.

Really, really happy.

NEITHER OF US mentioned sex as we got to his house. Or as he set the cat down, and we watched Sprinkles dart off.

She wasn't hissing.

Or scratching me.

So, she definitely seemed to like Bauther's territory more than mine.

"What are we making?" I asked him, as he opened his fridge.

"French Onion Chicken. Ever tried it before?"

"Nope. I don't even know what to think it would taste like."

"Like French Onion Soup, but better." He was pulling ingredients from the fridge one by one. "Want to help, or watch?"

My first instinct was to admit I'd rather just watch. Sitting down to rest my feet for a bit after spending so many hours working sounded blissful.

I was practically a professional when it came to ignoring my instincts, though.

"I'll help," I said.

He studied me for a minute, the fridge still open even though he'd stopped moving.

I bit my lip.

"You don't want to help," he said.

"It's fine," I insisted.

He closed the fridge and crossed the kitchen. When he reached me, he tucked a finger beneath my chin and used it to tilt my head back so our eyes met.

The touch was gentle, but dominant, in a way that made me hot.

"I want the truth, Si."

His eyes burned into mine.

I didn't want to be honest... but I did want to keep up with what we had going. And that probably required at least a little honesty.

So I admitted, "I don't want to cook. My feet hurt after work."

"Good. Sit down and watch me cook for you." He leaned in, and brushed his lips against mine. The kiss was soft, but lingering. Like he didn't want it to end any more than I did.

But eventually, he pulled away and stepped back.

I did the same.

And when he headed back to the fridge, I sat down on one of the barstools.

WE CHATTED WHILE HE COOKED.

I told him some of the ridiculous things Love, Tori, and I had done that we'd thought were rebellious back when we were kids living as glorified prisoners with the clan.

He told me how he'd ended up with all four of those master's degrees. Apparently, he just loved learning. History, in particular. One thing had turned into another when he didn't want to leave school, and didn't need the money to.

Shortly after the war ended, he found himself in Wildwood, and reluctantly agreed to be Madd's beta when the pack started growing. He and Madd had been leading the pack ever since, and he'd found himself in a number of humorous situations because of that.

After we ate together, I finally got out of my chair to clean up with him—despite his attempt at shooing me back to my seat.

I handed him the last pan, and he set to work drying it while I wiped down the sink with my sponge, then rinsed it out. Hesitation had me doing so slowly.

When there was no possible distraction left, I set the sponge back in the sink and turned around.

Bauther closed the cabinet door as I leaned my lower back against the sink, my elbows resting on the countertop. His eyes moved slowly down my body as he crossed the kitchen, meeting mine again as he reached me.

His hands captured my face, tilting my head back before his gaze searched mine.

A moment passed.

A long moment.

"What are you doing?" I finally whispered, though I wasn't entirely sure why I was whispering. Maybe because his hands felt incredible on my skin, and I was worried I could scare him away or something if I talked too loud.

Considering he was the beta of the largest wolf pack in the world, scaring him away with my voice didn't seem very realistic.

"Looking at you. I've never seen eyes this pretty before."

My face warmed. "They're just brown, Beck."

"Not *just* brown. They're the color of the forest floor after it rains. Fresh. Peaceful."

I bit my lip. "I don't know if *fresh* is a compliment."

His lips curved upward. "It is."

"How? Fresh isn't—"

He cut me off with his lips. They brushed mine lightly. Tentatively. Intimately.

It was soft and sweet.

But... I wanted more.

I slipped my tongue between his lips, and he parted for me without hesitation. His chest rumbled when my tongue stroked his, and he kissed me back slowly.

A minute went by.

Two.

Ten.

I didn't know. Everything blurred together as our mouths worked each other, tasting and exploring like there was nothing else we would rather be doing.

That was true for me.

There *wasn't* anything I would've rather been doing.

Eventually, my phone buzzed in my pocket. I jerked away from Bauther, yanked back to reality. My lips felt blissfully swollen, and my body was hot but relaxed.

"Sorry." I leaned against his chest, angling myself so I could pull the device from my back pocket.

"Don't apologize." His hands slid down to my shoulders before finding my waist and lingering there. I read the message, and sighed, dropping my phone on my counter. "What's wrong?"

"One of my coworkers went home sick. My boss needs me to work tomorrow."

"Tell her you're busy." His lips brushed mine lightly.

"I'm not, though."

"I can keep you busy." His hands slid down to my ass and squeezed lightly. My body clenched in response.

"I need the money."

"The pack will give you whatever you need. We have more cash than we know what to do with."

"I don't want to rely on the pack." I shook my head. "I still need to pay Tori back, anyway. She bought me a *car* pretty soon after I moved here. If I had another way to get around, I would've turned it down, but I didn't."

"Tori is mated to one of the oldest werewolves in the country. She doesn't need your money."

My defenses went up a little. "I know she doesn't need it, but it's the principle of the matter."

"Then pay her back." He squeezed my ass lightly.

I sent a quick message back to my boss that I'd be at work, then set my phone down on the counter. "Where were we?"

"I was waiting for you to take my clothes off, actually."

I smiled. "Were you?"

"Always." His lips curved upward.

"If you wait for me to make a move, you might be waiting forever, Beck."

"I've got nothing but time." He squeezed my ass again, and I arched against him enough to make him rumble. "You set the pace."

"You're the dominant one in this... relationship."

I wasn't sure what else to call it. And it *was* a relationship, even though it wasn't a serious one.

"Am I?" His eyes were playful, but I saw something in them.

Something like a challenge.

He wanted me to be in charge. I was really shitty at that, but maybe I could give it a try. I *had* been the one to deepen the kiss, and that was fun. Why couldn't I take over for a bit?

"Alright, take your shirt off," I said. Giving a command felt foreign, but I liked it.

His gaze heated, and he stepped back just enough to give himself space to peel the shirt over his head. I didn't look away from him as it hit the floor.

Damn, he was gorgeous.

Thick, chiseled muscles, everywhere.

Maybe I could get used to being in charge.

"Your pants, too," I said.

His eyes were hot as he unbuttoned them, then pushed the fabric down his thighs.

And holy hell, the man wasn't wearing underwear.

His cock was hard and huge, and my entire body flushed at the sight of it.

"Are you sure that will fit inside me?" The question slipped out before I could rethink asking it.

His chest rumbled again. "Not a fucking doubt."

I heated further. "Can I take your hair down?" It was up in a bun, and I'd never seen it loose.

"Don't ask, Si. Tell."

I bit my lip, insanely wet between my thighs. "Take your hair down."

He tugged it free, and the strands fell around his face. He was stunning. Absolutely stunning.

"It looks silky. Come here so I can touch it." I stumbled over the command a little, but he didn't mention it.

Instead, Bauther closed the small distance between us.

His erection pressed against my abdomen, and his hands landed on my hips again.

I slipped my hands into his hair, not surprised at all to find it just as soft as it looked. "How do you have better hair than me? This really isn't fair."

His eyes narrowed. "Your hair is perfect."

I tugged lightly on his hair. "Okay."

"Don't say things just to placate me, Sienna. That's not how this works."

"Why not?"

"We're equals. If you don't know that I find you beautiful, we don't take this any further until you do."

Damn.

As much fun as I'd been having while I was in charge, I liked it when he was dominant, too.

But ultimately, after the way things had happened the night before, I really didn't doubt his attraction to me. The man had spent hours touching me and tasting me.

So, if he said my hair was perfect, he honestly meant that he found it perfect.

"I believe you. You've made it way too clear that you're attracted to me for me not to."

There was satisfaction in his gaze. "Good."

I bit my lip. It was hot and swollen... like other parts of me.

I wanted more.

"Am I still in charge?" I asked, my hands still tangled in his hair.

"You're always in charge, Si."

I rolled my eyes.

His lips curved wickedly. "What do you want me to do to you?"

"What do *you* want to do to *me*?"

"Everything, and then some."

I rolled my eyes again, but couldn't hold back my small smile. He really wanted me to make the calls.

Though I was worried I'd say something wrong, or he'd wish I made a different choice, I forced my nerves down. "Take my clothes off, Beck."

His chest rumbled in satisfaction.

He lifted me up onto the countertop, then slowly peeled my sweater over my head. When the fabric hit the floor, his hands were sliding over the lace of my bra, feeling my breasts through the fabric.

My eyes closed, my breathing growing shallow and my head tipping back as he touched me. Soon enough, his hands found the clasp of my bra. He undid the binding, and it joined my sweater on the floor.

I gasped as his mouth found my breast.

His lips, teeth, and tongue worked my nipple slowly, until I was breathing hard, my hands tangled in his hair.

Bauther tugged me to the edge of the counter, his mouth moving down my abdomen until he found my leggings. His fingers hooked in the waistband, and he slowly peeled them down my thighs, leaving my thong where it was.

My chest rose and fell quickly as he lowered his face between my legs and looked up at me, meeting my eyes as he inhaled deeply. "You smell so fucking delicious."

My entire body clenched.

When he leaned in and caught the lace of my thong between his teeth, I couldn't hold back my soft moan.

He dragged it down my thighs and let it fall to the floor before he stood again, straightening to his full height. He was insanely tall, even with the countertop giving me a few extra inches, but I barely noticed his height. We were both way too naked to care about that.

"What now, Si?" His voice was low and growly. I had to clench my thighs to stop myself from wrapping my legs around his hips and pulling him close.

I was still breathing rapidly—too rapidly.

I wanted more.

I needed more.

"Lick me," I whispered.

His gaze was so damn hot. "Where?"

He was going to make me say it.

I was desperate enough that I didn't think twice about doing so. "My clit."

He made a noise of satisfaction before he kneeled down in front of me. His hands caught the backs of my legs, and he pulled me to the very edge of the counter as he opened me wide and gave me what I wanted.

I cried out as he licked my clit once, then again.

Slowly.

So, so slowly.

It was too much and not enough at the same time.

"Harder," I ordered, my voice desperate.

He rumbled, and the pressure increased as he continued working me. My fingers tangled in his hair again, probably knotting the smooth strands, but he didn't give a damn.

"Beck," I moaned, as I neared the edge of my climax. I wanted *more*. I needed *more*. "Your fingers. Use your fingers."

He released one of my thighs, and I cried out as he slid two fingers inside me.

I shattered, sounds of pleasure escaping me. My hips jerked and my body rocked as I gripped his hair for dear life.

When I came down from the high, his tongue was still working me. His motions were slower, giving me a chance to recover a little, but it wasn't enough.

"Fuck me," I said breathlessly, chest still rising and falling rapidly.

"Not yet." His mouth moved against my core, his fingers still buried inside me.

"I'm in charge, Beck," I said, before I could think about it. As the words left my lips, my body tensed, like it was waiting for him to react poorly to my statement.

His eyes met mine, hot and needy.

The tension in my middle eased just slightly.

"You're perfect," he rumbled against me.

Then, he slowly pulled away, dragging his tongue down the inside of my thigh as he let go. I felt the loss when he slid his fingers out of my channel, but wanted what was coming too desperately to react.

Beck—it seemed wrong to think of him as Bauther when he was about to be inside me—lifted me by my thighs. I released his hair, grabbing his shoulders as he carried me through the house. I'd never had a tour, so I didn't know exactly where we were headed, but I had a safe guess.

And it proved correct when he carried me right into his bedroom.

"The kitchen wasn't good enough?" I asked.

"Not for your first time."

I appreciated that, tremendously.

"You're still going to have to be in charge. I refuse to hurt you," he said, as he sat down on the bed and pulled me onto his lap. The length of his erection pressed against my clit, hot and hard.

I bit my lip, suddenly less sure than I'd been. Though I was still horny, pain didn't sound great.

His mouth caught mine before I could start overthinking anything, and our tongues met. I could taste my pleasure on his lips, and it made my toes curl.

All worries left my mind as we made out.

I gripped his hair again as I moved my hips, grinding against his cock.

His hands worked my breasts before sliding down to my ass.

Desire swelled within me, and I wanted more.

I wanted *him*.

Beck was so damn huge, I just had to ease away a little to find the head of his cock. I moaned into his mouth when it pressed against my entrance, and his grip on my ass tightened.

I lowered my weight over him, and he swore against my lips when the head of his cock finally pushed inside me.

My brain short-circuited at the feeling.

He was so hard.

So insanely thick.

So *hot*.

But it wasn't enough.

I gave myself a minute to adjust before I lowered myself further, taking a few more inches of him. There was a little resistance, and some pain, but I pushed through, crying out when I was past the worst of it.

He cursed against my mouth again, his voice strained and his grip tight. "You're a fucking dream, Si."

I was too overwhelmed, and breathing too fast, to reply.

But when I'd adjusted, I finally sank down the rest of the way. He bottomed out inside me, and our bodies were more connected than I'd ever imagined was possible.

And it felt *good*.

So intensely good.

"Holy shit," I moaned, my hips moving lightly as I sat on him.

"No kidding. You feel too good." His growl was low.

Almost animalistic.

I absolutely loved it.

I rocked my hips a little harder, and my breathing grew shallower.

He dragged his thumb over my clit, and I lost it.

Frantic cries escaped me as I jerked my hips, shattering on his cock. His chest rumbled low and loud as he watched me, leaving his thumb in place.

The climax was longer and harder than I could ever remember experiencing.

"You didn't come with me?" I asked, still panting as I tried to recover a little.

"No. I wanted to watch and feel your pleasure. You're so damn gorgeous."

My grip on his hair tightened. Supernatural guys could climax just as many times as women, so there was no reason for him not to get off when I did. "You lose it with me every time. *Every time.*"

His eyes were hot. "Alright."

He pressed his thumb against my clit lightly, and I swore, my hips jerking. "Take over, Beck. Make me feel good again."

He growled, and in one motion, had me on my back. His hands found my ass again, and he tilted us as he pulled out and drove into me slowly.

My cries were frantic as I shattered again, my body squeezing him with every wave of my pleasure.

Beck snarled, pumping into me harder. Despite my pleasure, my attention was locked on his face and body as he lost control inside me.

It was surreal.

So, so surreal.

And I wanted more.

Beck's movements slowed as he came down from his climax, but he didn't stop.

The ferocity in his gaze told me he didn't want to any more than I did.

When I hooked my legs around his ass and arched my back, he didn't waste any time giving me what I wanted—or taking what he wanted.

It was everything, and more.

SIENNA

IT WAS the middle of the night when I finally told Beck I should go home. We were both sweaty and sticky, but I was blissed-out in a way I'd never imagined.

He helped me into my clothes, grabbed my bag, then slipped his fingers between mine and walked me home. Neither of us said a word on the way back, but our sides were all but pressed together throughout the short walk.

He kissed me softly at my front door. When he pulled away, a thought occurred to me.

"Sprinkles is still at your house."

We hadn't heard a peep from her while we were there. Then again, we'd been *busy*.

"She's fine. We can try to take her back to your place tomorrow, when you get off work."

My lips curved at the blatant suggestion that we'd be together when I got off work. "Are you bringing me lunch again?"

"Of course. Making you dinner, too."

My smile widened. "Alright. See you tomorrow."

He kissed me again, then finally let me go.

I slipped into the house and locked the door behind me, leaning up against it with a dopey smile on my face.

Life was good. Insanely good.

I MADE my way into the bathroom, humming a song. I was too hyped-up to sleep, so a bath sounded nice, and I definitely needed to wash up.

While the water warmed, I took my clothes off and pulled my phone from my bag.

There were a million texts in the Wildwood Bitches group chat, so I pulled it up while I slipped into the tub.

The first thing I saw was a picture of me and Beck.

It had been taken a few minutes earlier, of us standing on my doorstep, kissing.

Holy shit.

I clenched my jaw as I read through the messages that followed it.

HOLLY

OMG THEY HAVE TO BE MATES

TAYLOR

I'm loving this

HANNAH

They're adorable!

BECCA

Totally mates

ASHLEY

Guess he's off the market for good

EMMEE

Sigh

MEGAN

Imagine how adorable their babies will be!

I halted when I read that.

Legitimately stopped breathing, absolutely freezing in place.

I'd had my IUD taken out when I got to Wildwood. The clan had forced us to have them put in, and I'd hated knowing that. Taking it out felt like freeing myself, as silly as that was.

But I also hadn't planned on having sex.

So I hadn't started any other method of birth control.

...Which was now looking like a very bad call.

Very.

Bad.

Call.

I immediately called Tori, but she didn't answer.

So I called Love.

"Hello?" Madd's voice was gravelly when he answered for her.

"I need to talk to Love," I squeaked.

There was a pause, and my friend answered. "Are you okay?"

"I don't know."

"Where are you? I'll kill Bauther," Love growled.

"No, it's not—he didn't—we had sex. It was good. Great. Incredible. But I'm home now, and I just realized we didn't use protection. I got my IUD out, and we didn't use condoms. I didn't think about it."

There was a moment of silence.

A long moment of silence.

"Shit," Love finally said.

"I know." I squeezed my eyes shut. "We're not mates, Love. A baby would complicate things."

"It takes some people a long time to get pregnant. You have to line it up right in your cycle to even make it a possibility, don't you?" Love asked.

Madd's voice was muffled, but I heard him clear enough when he said, "Fated shifter couples are extremely fertile.

The women joke about their fertility making up for how few of them there are. If a female shifter has unprotected sex with her mate, it's safe to assume there will be a baby."

My shoulders relaxed, and a relieved breath escaped me. "We're not mates, so I should be fine, right?"

Love was silent.

Madd was too.

"Hello?"

"Sienna," Love said, her voice tentative. "I need you to go to your blood stash and look for a bag of Bauther's. I'm sure he donated when we first moved here."

"Why do I need to do that?" There was fear in my voice.

I knew why.

I did.

I just refused to admit it.

"Just do it, and call me back when you're ready, okay? I love you. Everything's going to be fine."

She hung up the phone, and I squeezed my eyes shut.

Then I dropped my phone next to the tub.

The back of my head crashed against the wall. What the hell had I been thinking?

I'd been thinking with my vagina, obviously.

And it was a mistake. A huge one.

I took thirty seconds to wash myself off. Then I unplugged the drain, wrapped myself in a towel, and headed to my garage.

Where my blood freezers were.

The guys in the pack had all donated for Tori when she got to Wildwood, so there was an assload of blood. We hadn't gone through much of it before she mated with Vex, and mated blood wolves relied on their mate for blood.

So, the freezers were mine.

And they were very, very full.

I rolled the towel a few times so it wouldn't slide down my tits, and opened the first freezer.

There were names written in sharpie on the bags of blood.

Collin Fellop

Osten Jin

Warner Vegas

I pulled out bag after bag, piling them on the garage floor, one after another.

Halfway through the second freezer, I lifted a bag and halted.

Beckett Bauther

I stared down at his name for a moment.

A long, long moment.

"I don't want to do this," I finally whispered, to myself and to my wolf.

"We'll be okay," my wolf murmured back. *"Open the bag."*

I squeezed my eyes shut.

She already knew the answer to my question. She had to. She was just keeping quiet, letting me figure it out myself.

But, after another moment, I finally grabbed the bag and walked back into the house. The freezer was still open, and there were blood bags all over the garage, but they would survive a few minutes.

I needed to know.

The door to the garage shut behind me as I walked into the kitchen and pulled a pair of scissors from a drawer. I didn't bother warming the blood up. I didn't need it warm to know the truth.

I held my breath while I cut it open.

Setting the scissors down on the counter again, I finally lifted the bag to my nose and let myself inhale.

My entire body shuddered as his scent flooded my lungs.

My fangs descended instantly.

My body flushed, despite the hours we'd spent in bed together.

I dropped the bag in the sink and scrambled to turn the water on. It rained down over the blood, easing the ferocity of his scent just a little.

I watched the blood thaw and roll down the drain bit by bit, before I forced myself to admit the truth.

Beckett Bauther was my fated mate.

He knew it. He'd known it since the moment he kissed me, if not earlier.

And he'd kept the truth from me.

He'd touched me.

Tasted me.

Fucked me.

But he hadn't come clean about what he was to me.

"He could still be a good mate," my wolf whispered.

"He lied to me," I said.

My voice was flat.

Hollow.

My heart was, too.

And he wasn't the only one who had kept the truth from me. Love had known, and hadn't said anything.

I shut off the water and walked back to the bathroom. Picking up the phone, I calmly called Love back.

"Hey," she said.

"If you and Madd can keep a secret like that for him, you can keep one just as big for me. Don't say anything to him about what I told you."

"Sienna," Love protested.

"Give me your word. Both of you."

"I won't say anything." Love's voice was tight.

"Your business is between you and your mate," Madd agreed.

"Good. Just so you're aware, I'll be joining Vex's pack now, seeing as there's a conflict of interest between me and your beta. I don't need your protection anymore."

"Wait," Love started to argue.

I hung up before she had the chance to say anything, and let out a long breath.

Then, I reloaded the freezers, threw some clothes and blood bags in a duffel, and got in my car.

My gaze caught on Smith's as I drove away. He was sitting on my porch, keeping an eye on my house. He rotated my guard duty with Beck, but I rarely saw him. Bauther usually guarded me around the clock himself, sleeping in front of my house in his wolf form when necessary.

The fact that Smith was there after we'd spent hours in bed together felt like a slap in the face.

Beck didn't want me to realize what we were to each other, so he put Smith on duty. His wolf had to be driving him mad over the distance between us, but he still had Smith watching me, to help him hide the truth.

What a fucking *bastard*.

I flipped Smith off as I drove past him. There was no point in gunning the engine or trying to get away from him; I'd already told Madd where I was going.

So I seethed while he followed me down the back roads that led to Tori and Vex's place, cursing Beck's name the whole way there.

MY FIST RAPPED on the door loudly.

There was a moment of silence. They were probably asleep.

So I bit my lip, but rang the doorbell. Twice.

Heavy footsteps were on the floor a minute later, and Vex ripped the door open with a snarl on his face.

The snarl vanished when he saw me on his doorstep. "Sienna?"

"I need a place to stay." My voice was small, and wobbly.

My anger was fading too fast.

Vex opened the door wider, gesturing me inside. "Let me grab Tori."

I nodded, and he padded down the hallway. Everything in their house was brand new; he'd finished the final renovations a few weeks earlier. It had been in terrible shape when he moved in, but he'd made the place beautiful.

Tori came out in a tank top and shorts a minute later, her cheekbone-length strawberry-blonde hair a wreck. "What happened?"

"I had sex with Bauther," I blurted. "And I realized when I got home that we didn't use protection. When I called Love to ask if that would be a problem, she told me to pull his blood from my freezer. She *knew* we were mates, and she didn't tell me. And Madd said female werewolves are super fertile, so now I could get *pregnant*, and Beck *lied* to me, he has to know we're mates, and—"

Tori pulled me into her arms for a tight hug. I squeezed her back fiercely, panic and anger and sadness still coursing through me. "Breathe, Sienna."

I took a deep breath in.

She led me to the couch and pulled me down to sit next to her. "Now, start from the beginning."

I let out a long, staggered breath, but told her everything.

Well, not *everything*, everything. She didn't need to know the details about the sex, and she didn't ask for them.

Vex was on the other side of the couch, his arms folded and his brows drawn together when I finally finished the story.

Tori's eyes were wide, and she ran a hand through her tousled hair. "Damn, that's a mess."

"I know." My voice was miserable. "What do I do?"

"Well, you know you can always stay with us. We have a spare room with your name on it. The guys are working on a few more houses right now, but none of them are in great shape yet. I think it'll be at least a week or two before one's ready for anyone to attempt living in it." Tori looked at Vex.

"At least three," Vex said.

Which meant at least three weeks of living with a newly-mated couple who were all over each other constantly.

Lovely.

It was better than the alternative of going back to Love's pack after she kept the truth from me.

"The question is, what are you going to do when your mate shows up at my door?" Vex asked, gesturing toward the front of the house.

Tori grimaced. "You think he'll come here?"

"I think he'll be here in the next ten minutes," Vex said bluntly.

Tori's grimace deepened.

"As far as he knows, he's keeping up with his façade," I argued. "Hiding the truth from me. I—"

"Smith would've called him the second you drove away. His wolf won't let him sleep when he's apart from you, so he would've already been awake. And it wouldn't take long for him to stop at your house, find the empty blood bag in your sink, and put two and two together. He's probably on his way here right now," Vex countered.

Shit.

Vex's logic was too sound.

I was in way over my head.

And what would I do if Beck really tracked me all the way to Tori's house? I wouldn't do what he wanted, of course. I wouldn't go back to Love's pack. I wouldn't act like the bastard hadn't lied to me from the beginning. I couldn't *trust* him.

"I don't know what I'll do," I admitted.

"I'll kick his ass for you," Tori said bluntly. "And we'll figure out what we're doing about the whole situation while he's hobbling home, licking his wounds."

Vex snorted. "Bauther's playing the long game with his mate. Most male wolves can't manage it. I sure as fuck couldn't. He's not going to walk away from her."

"But—" Tori began.

A harsh knock on the front door cut her off.

She looked at me.

I looked at her.

We both looked at Vex.

He lifted his hands. "I'm not getting involved. If I keep the Wildwood beta from his mate, the pack legally has the right to rain hell down on us."

Tori glowered at him. "I'm going to kick *your* ass."

"Sounds like fun."

There was another knock at the door. A louder one.

"Maybe I should escape out the back?" I suggested, easing to my feet.

"No," Tori and Vex barked at the same time.

My gaze jerked between them.

Tori pointed at the couch. "Stay there."

Then, she stormed to the door.

I sat back down as she yanked it open.

"Where is she?" Beck's voice was low and dangerous.

"Safe, with people who haven't kept very important truths from her while *fucking her*," Tori shot back. "Go home."

She tried to slam the door shut, but Beck caught it and stepped past her, into the house.

I couldn't stop my sharp breath in when I saw him.

He was shirtless and shoeless, wearing nothing but a pair of basketball shorts that looked like they'd been through the ringer. He must've run all the way there in his wolf form.

His hair was just as messy as I'd left it, hanging loose and tangled.

Somehow, he was even sexier now that I knew he was supposed to be my mate.

"Get out of my house!" Tori tossed a hand toward the front door, which was standing open.

Beck ignored her. His gaze moved up and down my body before he was satisfied that I was okay. Even then, he didn't look at Tori. He stared at me.

"We need to talk."

"It's a little late for talking, don't you think?" My voice was tight.

"No."

"It was a rhetorical question, asshole." Tori put a hand on his bicep long enough to shove him toward the front door. He didn't budge, of course.

My wolf stirred in my chest, and a loud growl rattled the room.

Tori halted.

Beck's eyes gleamed.

"Let go of the beta, Tor." Vex's voice was smooth, but there was a low undertone. I wasn't sure if it was his possessiveness, or his worry that my wolf might take over and attack her for touching my mate.

Tori released Beck's arm instantly, but didn't step back. "This is our pack's territory, Bauther. Storming in uninvited might as well be a declaration of war."

"Hiding my mate from me is far more damning than encroaching your territory. Wouldn't you agree, Vex?"

Beck's words were even, and his gaze didn't flick to the alpha as he spoke.

"In most situations, yes. Considering your mate asked my mate—her sister in all but blood—for sanctuary after you lied to her, it could go either way in court." Since Vex was part of the supernatural government, it seemed safe to assume he was pretty well-versed on the laws.

"I didn't *lie* to her."

"A lie by omission is still a lie," Tori growled.

"I didn't know for sure that she was my mate until two days ago. Two days is a very reasonable amount of time to wait before admitting the truth when one knows their female isn't looking for a male," Beck said.

I looked at Vex.

He looked at Tori. "He has a point. There's likely no court that would side with us on keeping him from her."

"I don't give a damn about courts," Tori hissed, her attention jerking back to Beck. "I *knew* you were wrong for Sienna. Even *Ox* wouldn't hide the truth from her like this. I—what the hell are you doing?"

Beck stepped past her, striding toward me.

I tried to shrink back into the couch, and failed horribly.

"Keeping up with the tradition of abducting my blood wolf." He scooped me up off the couch, and I glared at him, though I didn't try to fight my way free.

I was smart enough to know that was a fight I didn't stand a chance at winning.

"Goodnight. You can call Sienna in the morning," Bauther said over his shoulder.

"She won't forgive you for this," Tori huffed, following us out of the house.

Beck pulled my keys out of my bag and got the door open quickly, leaving me on his lap while he started the engine and called out, "You forgave Vex. Love forgave Madd. The odds are on my side."

With that, he shut the door.

And drove off, with me *still* on his lap.

seven

BAUTHER

MY HEART PUMPED HARD, my chest rising and falling unevenly as I hauled ass away from Vex's place.

I could've lost her.

I could've lost Sienna.

I could've lost my *mate*.

My plan to win her heart slowly was out the fucking window.

I was never letting her out of my sight again.

"Driving with me on your lap doesn't seem safe," Sienna said, her lips moving against my neck.

My cock hardened with her touch, the scent of her thick in my lungs and on my skin.

"I'm being careful." The words came out a growl. It was getting harder to suppress my emotions. I nearly lost my shit when I got the call from Smith that she'd taken off, and the stress was catching up with me.

"No one's careful enough to drive with someone on their lap. Especially when they're already *hard*."

"I've been hard for months, Si. You'll be fine."

She huffed, but stopped arguing with me.

My conscience bugged me though.

Before I turned onto the first main road we came across, I pulled over. Sienna lifted her head when I put the car in park, and I stepped out of the vehicle, carrying her with me. When I set her down on the passenger seat, she looked grudgingly grateful.

I buckled her seat belt for her, then closed her door and took the driver's seat again. Both of us were silent as I turned onto the street, and as I wove through the city.

She finally spoke as we neared the pack's neighborhood. "We're not having sex again."

I blinked.

That wasn't what I'd expected to hear, though it didn't exactly surprise me.

"I trusted you," she added. "You broke my trust. I won't let it happen again."

That stung.

"You didn't want a mate," I said. "I heard that loud and clear. I kept my distance as much as my wolf would allow, until he gave me no choice."

"You *asked me out* in a *bar*. That's a far cry from your wolf forcing you to grab me and kiss me."

"Ox is in town. The alphas wanted to pair you with him. He would've talked you into his bed; there are *legends* about how many mated women he's talked into his bed. You'd never paid any of the other males a moment of attention, but I wasn't risking it with him."

"So you talked me into *your* bed instead," she said flatly.

"You're mine." I couldn't stop myself from growling the words. "And let's not pretend last night was only about me. I got you off half a dozen times, Si."

When I glanced at her through my rearview mirror, I found her face bright red. "You're an ass."

"I'm aware." I dragged my hair away from my face. It was a damn mess, but it smelled so strongly of her pleasure that I wasn't about to drag a brush through it. I wanted as much of her scent on me as possible. "Keeping it quiet while we bonded seemed like the best call at the time."

"The best call for *you*. Not for me."

"You didn't want a mate," I repeated. "I showed you at least a few of the benefits."

When I looked at her again, her face was even redder.

She was pissed, unsurprisingly.

"You showed me the benefits for your own damn sake."

"Of course I did. I've been waiting to meet you for centuries. I wasn't going to just let you go because you didn't see how a mate could benefit you."

She fell silent at that.

I'd seen her duffel bag in the back seat of her car, so I didn't bother taking her to her house. Considering the way she'd tried to get away from me, she was moving into my place. It was bigger, and tucked away in the corner of the neighborhood, where we had more space and privacy.

"You should've asked me whether I was your mate instead of digging out that damn blood bag," I said, my jaw clenching. "You could've called me, or walked back over. I would've told you the truth if you asked me."

"I didn't want the truth. I wanted casual sex." Her gaze was trained outside.

I forced my breathing to remain even, despite the anger building within me. "Casual sex is nothing like what I gave you. If you hooked up with a stranger, he wouldn't focus on your pleasure. He wouldn't enjoy spending hours with his mouth on you. He would use you, then walk away."

"And you don't think you used me at all?" she shot back.

"Of course not. I focused on you without asking for anything in return. What you gave me, you gave because you wanted to."

"Stop. Just stop, okay? I'm done."

I clenched my jaw, but stayed silent through the rest of the drive.

When I pulled into the garage and closed it behind us, she didn't make a move to get out.

She looked straight ahead as she said, "Since you've abducted me, what are your ground rules?"

"There aren't any *rules*."

She scoffed.

"You can do anything you want, Si. You're free. You'll just have me tailing you, the same way you did before you realized what we are to each other. And you'll come home to this house we share, rather than to your own place. You're safer here."

"I'm not sharing a bed with you."

"I didn't expect you to. There's a spare bedroom. It's yours."

She relaxed slightly. "Fine. Where is it?"

"Across the hall from mine. I'll grab your bag."

She slipped out of the car while I pulled her duffel off the back seat. I caught her in the hallway, and followed her into the room. It wasn't massive, but it wasn't tiny, and I already had a bed set up with sheets and blankets.

"Dammit," Sienna grumbled as soon as she stepped into the room.

"What?" I asked, though my eyes landed on the reason for her curse the moment I passed through the door.

Sprinkles was on the spare bed.

"She'll kill me if I try to sleep there," Sienna said.

"She likes me. You can take my room until she decides to move."

"I'm not taking your room, Bauther."

She called me Beck when she wasn't pissed at me.

"It smells so much like you that I won't be able to sleep anyway. It's yours." Without waiting for a disagreement, I carried her bag into my room and set it down on the end of the bed.

When I unzipped it to start putting her things away, I halted, staring down into the duffel.

There were bags of blood in it. On top of her clothes.

Charlie Tobin's blood.

Hershel Ott's blood.

Login Jacob's blood.

"You didn't drink mine after you opened the bag?" My voice strained as I struggled not to growl at her again.

"Of course I didn't. I would be addicted to you if I drank your blood." She took the bags, and another half dozen beneath them. "If you get rid of them so I'm forced to drink from you, I won't forgive you."

"I would never do that."

"I don't believe you." Her bluntness was fucking painful.

I was glad she told me the truth, though.

Painful truth was a hell of a lot more important than kind lies.

Which, in hindsight, was what I'd given her.

A kind lie that we could have casual sex without being mates.

I hadn't *technically* lied, but I had kept the truth from her. I should've listened to everyone who told me that was a shitty idea.

"I'm sorry," I admitted to her. It was the truth. "If I could go back and smack myself upside the head for not telling you the moment I caught your scent in that bar, I would do it. And I'd tell you the truth."

"In the bar?" Her gaze was critical, like she didn't believe me.

"I planned on asking you out as soon as I learned Ox was coming to meet you. I hoped I'd learn if you were my mate when I did. You washed the lotion and perfume off your hands, so I finally caught a hint of your scent beneath the soap's smell. That confirmed what you were to me."

"You really didn't know before that?"

"No." It was the truth. "I've suspected since the first time I met you, but I was trying to give you space. Just protecting you settled my wolf for the most part."

She stepped out of the room with her blood bags. When she came back a few minutes later, I assumed they were in the freezer. And while I'd itch like mad to throw them out, I knew I had no real option but to leave them for her.

When she decided to drink from me, it had to be on her terms. But she *would* decide to drink from me eventually, even if I had to spend the next few months or years proving to her that I was trustworthy first.

"If there are no rules, I can do whatever I want," she said casually.

"Yes."

"Perfect."

Her bitter smile told me I wasn't going to like the reason she'd asked for clarification on that.

Her phone was to her ear a heartbeat later. After a short pause, she said, "Hi, Madd."

My forehead creased.

"I heard there's an alpha in town to meet me. Ox, right? I'm ready to set up that date."

My wolf snarled.

I nearly did too.

"Oh, don't worry about Beck. He says there are no rules, so I can do whatever I want. Including meet other men, in hopes of finding a mate who might actually tell me the truth."

We snarled together at that.

Her defiant gaze collided with mine, her eyes daring me to disagree. To tell her she wasn't free to do *that*.

And I wanted to.

Fuck, I wanted to.

But something told me I would regret it if I did.

"Fine. Here he is." Her voice was clipped as she crossed the distance between us and handed me the phone.

I accepted it, my entire body tense.

"You want me to agree to this?" Madd asked. He sounded tired. "I really don't want you killing him. I'd rather avoid a pack war, and we'll need their backup if any more vamps come after our females."

"I told her she's free," I gritted out. "Set up the meeting."

I couldn't call it a date.

Not if I wanted to retain my sanity.

Madd sighed. "Fine."

Sienna held her hand out for the phone, and I forced myself to give it back to her. "Tomorrow night works," she said. "It'll be fun. Thanks."

I'd kill the bastard if he so much as touched her hand, but sure, *fun* was a good description.

She hung up the phone and tucked it into her pocket, daring me to argue.

I clenched my jaw to stop myself from doing exactly that.

My wolf all but roared at me to do something, and I forced myself to ignore him and stay in my human form.

"I need to work early," Sienna said, gesturing toward the door.

She wanted me out.

Right.

I jerked my head in a nod, and left the room. She shut the door hard behind me, and I heard the lock twist immediately.

Damn, I'd screwed up.

eight

SIENNA

I THOUGHT I was too worked up to sleep, but I was so exhausted, I crashed the moment my head hit the pillow.

My phone's alarm woke me up way too early, and I stumbled into the shower. After a quick rinse to wake me up, I threw my hair up in a ponytail and pulled on a pair of clothes.

My stomach was growling, so I stepped into my shoes and grabbed my purse, then opened the bedroom door.

Though I planned on digging something to eat out of Beck's fridge, I halted in the doorway.

Because there was a man sprawled out on the ground. A gorgeous man.

Right in front of my door.

He was snoring lightly, and Sprinkles was draped over his chest, also asleep.

Shit.

For a minute, I just stared at the two of them. Beck was shirtless, wearing the same basketball shorts from the night before. They did absolutely nothing to hide his morning wood. If anything, they highlighted it.

Which made me warm, even if I didn't want to admit it.

And he was asleep on the floor, for some reason.

With Sprinkles—vicious, horrible Sprinkles—asleep on him and clearly not doing any damage.

Then again, laying on his bare chest would probably erase my anger too. It had to be the world's most perfect chest.

I forced myself to let out a slow breath, hoping it would center me.

It didn't.

I was severely shaken up by everything I'd learned. The mate thing was huge, and infuriating—but the possibility of pregnancy?

Terrifying.

Absolutely terrifying.

I was planning to get the number for the pack's OB/GYN from Love as soon as she was up, but she wasn't working that day, so I assumed she would sleep in.

And the more information I had and learned, the more real everything was going to feel.

Reality was shit.

So, maybe I didn't want to learn anything.

Maybe I'd wait to call the gynecologist until more time had passed.

Or... well, maybe I should see if she knew more than Madd. Maybe I wouldn't be crazy fertile with Beck unless we sealed a mate bond or something.

It didn't hurt to be hopeful, right?

I finally forced myself to take a large, quiet step over the snoring pair on the floor, and made it without a problem. While I hunted through the fridge, I stayed quiet, so they wouldn't wake up.

Of course, just as I was finishing the bowl of cereal I'd poured myself, Beck came shuffling out of the hallway.

I forced my attention to remain on the cereal.

"Where's your phone?" His voice was more rumbly in the morning, which gave me goosebumps.

"Don't worry about it." I didn't look at him.

If I looked at him, I'd want him.

"I'm just going to charge it for you. I don't have the code, so I can't snoop," he said. "You have to leave soon. A few minutes is better than nothing."

I let out a slow breath, but handed it to him.

He was right.

And he must've noticed there wasn't a charger in my duffel bag when he started unpacking it the night before. I'd forgotten to grab one in my hurry to get away from him.

He grabbed a bowl and a spoon, and I couldn't stop my eyes from moving over his back.

He was too nice to look at.

And his hair was still tangled and messy from the night before, which satisfied some animalistic part of me.

I looked away when he started turning around, so he wouldn't catch me staring at him, and took another bite.

He padded across the kitchen and sat down next to me, pouring his own bowl of cereal. We ate together in silence, until the clock told me it was finally time to make my escape.

I unplugged my phone and slipped out of the house.

Beck didn't ask me to stop, or to drive with him. Something told me he'd assumed I'd say no.

Which I would've.

...Even though I'd want to say yes. I hated driving.

BECK CAUGHT up to me in his truck halfway through the drive. I couldn't stop myself from staring at him in my rearview mirror every time I hit a red light. He was too pretty.

And everything was so uncertain.

So up in the air.

Plus, he had lied to me. Or at least concealed the truth. Despite his apology, that still pissed me off, even though my anger was fading to a sort of resigned sadness.

Like usual, he sat in the front part of the bakery while I got to work. Though I knew I would see him if I looked in that direction, I refused to do so. He didn't need any encouragement after the way he'd kept the truth from me. I needed to put space between us.

Lots and lots of space.

Which was going to be pretty damn difficult if I really did get pregnant. Love had mentioned before that any kids the three of us had would be blood wolves like us. That meant my baby would be in even more danger than I was. On top of that, I'd never even imagined myself as a mom.

What if I was shitty at it?

What if I hated it?

What if I *loved* it?

My thoughts and emotions churned all morning, though I tried to chat with my coworkers like I usually did. Tori and Love weren't there, so the shallow chitchat was more diffi-cult than usual.

When my break finally came around, I slipped into the tiny breakroom and shut the door behind me, then pulled my phone from my pocket. I texted Love to ask for the

OB/GYN's number, and she sent it over immediately with a heart, and an apology.

I ignored both the apology and heart.

I would talk to her soon enough, and grudgingly forgive her, because we were basically family. There was probably a reason she'd kept the truth from me, as much as it pissed me off that she had.

Letting out an unsteady breath, I hit the button to call the doctor.

It rang a few times before she answered. "Hi, this is Susan DeMar."

"Hi, Susan," I said quickly. "I got your number from Love Madden. My name is Sienna. I'm one of the blood wolves in town, and I just had a few questions."

"Go right ahead." Her voice was warm. I didn't know much about her, but I knew she never participated in the *Wildwood Bitches* group chat. And I didn't think she would dare gossip about people's sexual histories and questions. If she did, she probably wouldn't survive long in a town full of werewolves.

"I was never taught much about a werewolf's fertility, or a blood wolf's. Assuming I accidentally had unprotected sex with my fated mate, what are the odds that it would lead to pregnancy?"

"There hasn't been much studying done on blood wolves, since making you is illegal." Her voice was neutral, which made me feel better. She wasn't mocking me or judging me, at least. "I only know of one blood wolf who's free and mated right now, and she has six kids, so it seems safe to assume you're as fertile as the rest of us. For a female werewolf either born or turned by her mate, unprotected sex pretty much guarantees pregnancy. I'd never say it's 100%, but it's close."

I squeezed my eyes shut.

Shit on a cracker.

"You can come in for labs in about two weeks, to find out for sure."

"That would be great," I whispered.

"I'll have my receptionist text you to schedule it. Whatever happens, it's going to be okay, Sienna. Your mate won't leave you to deal with anything alone."

That was kind of what I was afraid of.

I thanked her and ended the call, then leaned back against the chair and squeezed my eyes shut. They were stinging, but I hoped they would calm down soon. I needed to go back out to work in a few minutes.

My phone vibrated with a message, and I forced my eyes open.

BAUTHER

Where are you?

ME

Break room. Be out in a few.

He sent a thumbs-up, and I dropped my phone on my lap, running a hand over my face.

It was going to be a long two weeks.

WHEN LUNCHTIME CAME AROUND, my phone buzzed again.

> BAUTHER
>
> I brought food

I nearly groaned aloud.

Not because I didn't want to see him—but because I did, and I didn't want to let go of my anger yet.

I closed myself in the break room before replying.

> ME
>
> Grabbed my own, sorry

I hadn't brought anything, but I got free baked goods every shift I worked. So, I had two ham and cheese croissants for lunch most days. Love had gotten me addicted to them.

Usually, I grabbed a sugary coffee from the coffee shop portion of our bakery to go with them.

My phone buzzed again, but I ignored it.

I wasn't in the mood to talk to Beck, or to shoot him down anymore.

Two minutes passed in blissful silence before there was a quick knock on the breakroom door, and my coworker stuck her head in.

The look in her eyes was star-struck, and my stomach clenched.

I knew exactly who was behind that.

"Um, Beckett Bauther is claiming to be your mate. I hope you don't mind, but I let him back here…" she trailed off.

You would think she'd be used to seeing him in the front of the house, keeping an eye on me almost every day, but no.

The door opened, and he stepped past her briskly.

My wolf snarled when my coworker leaned in, brushing her chest against his side as he moved.

I couldn't stop myself from standing and stepping up against him—and he didn't try to stop himself from wrapping his arm around my waist and brushing his lips to mine. The kiss made me flush—and it made me want more.

"Thanks," Beck said, without looking back at her.

The man was clearly dismissing her. As much as I wanted to be pissed at him, I grudgingly appreciated that. He wanted it to be clear that he was mine.

"No problem. Have fun!" She closed the door behind herself.

Neither of us moved for a moment.

The smell of coffee cut through Beck's incredible scent, and my nostrils flared. "You brought drinks?"

"Yep." He lifted his arm that wasn't wrapped around me, revealing a bag of food and a drink carrier with two coffee cups in it. "It was a late night."

I couldn't stop the way my body flushed at the reminder of what we'd done.

Somehow, I'd managed to give him my virginity, discover he was my mate, and possibly get pregnant with his baby in one night.

One damn night.

If that wasn't bad luck, what was?

Then again, the first part hadn't been bad luck. Not even a little. Even while forcing myself to be angry, I couldn't pretend to hate that part.

I gestured for him to take the seat across from the small couch, just so I wouldn't have to sit next to him.

His skin would feel way too good against mine for me to risk that.

He handed me a coffee cup as I sat back down on the couch, then took the seat I'd pointed him to. "I'd already bought the food."

"I have croissants." I lifted one of them in the air to show him.

"I'll trade you, then. One croissant for one burger." He lifted the bag of food.

My stomach rumbled at the mention of the burger. "Are there fries too?"

"Of course. I'm not a heathen."

My lips curved upward. I couldn't stop them.

"He'll be a good dad for our pup," my wolf murmured.

"Shush. We are not having his pup." My smile faded at the thought. "Alright." I lifted my hand to toss the croissant to him, but he stood up instead.

And walked over to the couch, taking the seat next to me.

Damn him.

My wolf made a noise of satisfaction. *"He's good."*

"He's the worst."

She snorted.

We both knew I was lying.

He wasn't the worst.

I was sad that he'd kept the truth from me, and terrified about what the future held, but I'd been through too much shit to believe he was terrible.

I could've done so much worse.

If I'd ended up fated to any of the vampires in the clan that made me, my life would've been literal hell.

So, just the fact that he cared about protecting me and keeping me from harm made him much better than he could've been.

He took the croissant I'd already bitten into instead of the one in my hand, then set a box of takeout food on my lap. "I'll make dinner again tonight. We're meeting Ox for drinks."

Shit, I'd forgotten.

Why had my stubborn streak kicked in like that? Despite my anger, I didn't want to go out with the other guy. I'd only called Madd to figure out whether or not he was telling the truth about my freedom.

"What do you mean, we? It's a *date*," I said.

"I'm aware." Beck didn't look nearly as annoyed about it as he should've been, which made me suspicious. He bit into his croissant, and nodded. "These are good."

"You've never had one of Love's croissants before? She's obsessed with them."

"No."

"Well, you've been missing out." I took a bite of my own before I opened the box of takeout food. My mouth immediately watered at the sight of it.

Maybe I didn't like croissants as much as I'd been trying to convince myself I did.

I abandoned the bread and grabbed my burger, not wasting a minute before I took a bite. My groan filled the room, and all thoughts of my date that night vanished while I inhaled the food.

When I finished the burger and moved on to the fries, I finally looked up.

Beck's gaze was fixed on me, hot and heavy.

I paused, my fry only an inch from my parted lips.

He was staring at me.

How long had he been staring at me?

I glanced at his hand and found his croissant only half gone. He hadn't opened his burger.

And his erection raged against the front of his sweats, thick and hard and absolutely impossible not to see.

My body flushed.

I forced my hand to put the fry in my mouth.

I was immune to his attractiveness. Absolutely, completely immune.

My body was *very* warm, though.

And I was definitely getting wet between my thighs.

Which meant I needed to leave, before I did something I might regret. And things I might regret included everything that would lead to any kind of sex.

So I stood abruptly. "I've got to get back to work. Thanks for the trade."

Beck blinked.

His forehead creased.

I strode out of the room and back to my workstation before he had time to ask why my lunch was so much shorter that day.

And thankfully, he let me go without an argument.

nine

SIENNA

I SLIPPED OUT to my car a few minutes early, just so Beck wouldn't have time to catch me and hold my door. Or ask how my day had been. I was too tired to keep my mouth shut, and a little worried I might melt into him or something.

He caught up to me soon enough, following me home in his truck. Tori called while I drove home, thankfully distracting me so I didn't spend the whole drive trying to catch glimpses of him in my rearview mirror.

"So, how is it?" she asked.

"How is what?" I stopped at a red light and caught myself trying to stare at him. Scowling, I shook my head.

"Having a mate."

"If I wanted a mate, it would be nice. He brought me coffee and food. Knew my favorite drink, even."

She whistled. "Good man."

"I know." I let out a long breath. "I'm trying to stay mad at him, but it's hard. He's so pretty."

"Girl, I have the same problem. They distract you with their good looks. It's a thing."

I bit my lip to stop my smile. "Dammit."

"I know." There was a pause. "Did you call the pack's OB?"

My smile faded. "Yeah. She thinks it's pretty likely. I can't go back to find out for two more weeks."

"Shit."

"I'm trying to wrap my mind around the possibility, which is difficult. And then Beck's there, feeding me and acting like he didn't hide the truth. I don't know what to think or do anymore."

"I'm sorry. I know the situation isn't ideal."

"Plus, I was really pissed last night and had this awful idea to go out with Ox to get revenge on Beck. I called Madd to set it up, and Beck told him to do it. But during lunch, he made it sound like *we're* going on a date, not like *I'm* going out."

"Oh, honey, there's no way he's letting you go on that date alone. I'd be surprised if he hasn't already called Ox to tell him he's meeting a mated woman. Ronin has told me some stories about that man, and he sounds like a real piece of work."

"Like I said, it was a terrible idea."

"You know, you *can* still get out of it."

"No. I need to go, and try to be flirty. I'm supposed to be making Beck hurt the way he hurt me."

"Try not to sound so excited about it," Tori teased me.

I sighed. "I'm not good at revenge."

"I think that's actually a great quality, Sienna. If you flirt with Ox, there's a decent chance a fight breaks out. Bauther is only a beta because he respects Madd, not because he's not dominant enough."

"He's way less forceful than Madd or Ronin," I protested. "Even the way he puts his foot down about things is like... calm."

"That's more about personality than power."

I grimaced.

She wasn't wrong.

"I'm pulling into the driveway, and Beck's right behind me. We'll have to talk later."

"Alright. Love you!"

"Love you."

We both hung up, and I dropped my phone on the passenger seat before I started putting my car in park.

Beck pulled up onto the driveway next to me and rolled down his window. When he said something to me, I reluctantly rolled mine down too.

"Park in the garage. There's plenty of room," he called out.

"Alright."

Despite my grimace, I pulled into the opposite side of the garage from his truck. There were three spots, so he was right—there was plenty of room.

Beck came over and opened my door while I was grabbing my bag off the seat.

I stepped outside, and halted when I realized how close I was to him.

My nostrils flared as his scent washed over me.

He sort of smelled like... me.

"He hasn't washed our scent from his hair," my wolf said, her voice thick with approval. *"Good mate."*

"Good mates would practice proper hygiene," I grumbled.

She snorted at me.

We both knew how much we liked knowing he hadn't cleaned us off his hair or skin. It satisfied the territorial streak that we didn't like but couldn't escape.

"You should shower before we go," I said, ducking beneath his arm and leaving him to close my door as I strode toward the house.

He caught up to me in time to grab the door into the garage, holding that open for me too. "I'm not showering while you're not touching me."

"You're going to stink, then," I tossed back.

"I can think of many worse things than stinking of my mate's pleasure."

His words sent goosebumps over my arms.

Damn him.

Did I really want him walking into the bar smelling like my pleasure? Or dropping me off for my date while smelling like that?

Hard pass.

"If you wash your hair before I leave, I'll hug you," I said, still walking toward his bedroom, which I'd sort of claimed. "Then you'll smell like me in a more wholesome way."

"What's not wholesome about smelling like sex?" his voice was... playful.

And I found myself fighting a smile. "Just take a shower."

He chuckled. "Alright. Let me grab my stuff out of the closet."

Beck strode past me as I went to my duffel bag, which was still on the end of the bed. I hadn't brought any of my toiletries, which kind of sucked. I was going to smell like a man for my shitty date.

"We should probably drive separately, since I'm going out with Ox," I remarked, as he headed out with his clothes.

"That's fine."

My eyebrows lifted at the calmness in his voice.

Something told me I needed to be very, very suspicious.

"It is?"

"Probably for the best, if Ox is your date. I asked Belle to even out the numbers, so she'll either be there with him or me. Your call."

I saw red.

Fucking red.

My wolf snarled, and I did too, before I could stop myself.

There was a wicked gleam in Beck's eyes when I forced my breathing to even out.

"Great," I managed to grind out. "She's perfect for you."

The wickedness vanished. "No, she's not."

"Then you probably shouldn't have asked her out."

I turned away from him, fighting my emotions. They were strong. Way too strong, and I wasn't sure what to do or think about them.

He muttered something under his breath that sounded like a curse.

A moment later, his hands were on my hips, easing me away from the bed and turning me around. Then, they found my face, cupping my cheeks as his gorgeous eyes bore into mine.

As ridiculous as it was, mine were stinging a little.

I wanted to wipe them, but thought that might make the damn tears worse.

"I already asked Belle to go as Ox's date, and let him know earlier that you're mine. No one there will be under any impression that either of us is on the market. Both of us are taken, permanently. End of story."

"I'm not yours," I whispered, not sure I believed the words.

Beck's lips curved upward slightly. "You are. No doubt about it." He dragged his thumb slowly over my bottom lip, and I fought the urge to take it in my mouth. "I was trying to get a rise out of you. It was a shitty move. I'm sorry."

"You hurt me when you kept the truth from me, Beck."

His small smile vanished, his expression growing grave. "I know. If I could take it back, I would in a heartbeat. I'm sorry."

"Stop apologizing."

"What else would you like me to do? You're keeping me at an arm's length. You're not letting me touch you, and you're not talking to me the way you did."

"I talked to you that way because you *weren't* my mate."

"You talked to me that way because you were letting yourself like me, Si. Let yourself like me again."

"I need to process everything first. I'm not ready to be mated, okay? I only agreed to the date to show you how badly you hurt me, and now, I'm supposed to meet with some random pushy guy while acting like what? Like you and I are mates? I don't even know what that would mean for us." I pushed his hands off my face and took a step back.

"Leave Belle and Ox to each other, then. Stay here with me. Let me show you what it could mean."

"I'm not talking about sex, Beck. You showed me very thoroughly what that would be like. I'm talking about having an actual relationship. Sharing a life. Living together. Dealing with each other for the rest of forever. Maybe even having kids." I couldn't stop the last bit from slipping out.

Thankfully, he didn't seem to think much of it.

"I wasn't talking about sex either." His gaze was steady enough that I actually kind of believed him.

Then again, I'd believed he wasn't my mate too, so I obviously didn't have the best judgment.

"We can spend tonight talking, playing cards, and taking turns sharing our thoughts about what we want this to look like." He gestured between us.

I was tired of fighting with him, and hiding my feelings.

And I needed to hear what he had to say.

So, I agreed. "Alright. We can shower, then meet in the living room."

"I'll let Ox and Belle know."

I nodded, and he stepped back. His eyes were on me as he slipped out of the room, closing the door behind himself.

I took a moment to lock it before I let out a pent-up breath.

What had I just agreed to?

I TOOK a long time in the shower, avoiding the inevitable for as long as possible. Beck's hair products were nicer than mine, so I spent way too long breathing in their scents and marveling over how soft they were making my hair.

By the time I finally put on a pair of comfortable shorts and a soft sleep t-shirt, I'd decided I couldn't avoid him any longer, and padded to the door.

As soon as I cracked it open, I paused. My stomach growled as I inhaled deeply, catching a whiff of whatever was cooking.

Some kind of Italian food.

Yummm.

I took another deep breath in and forced myself to keep moving. The scent of Beck's shampoo filled my lungs and made my body warmer as I walked.

I needed serious help. Two nights of sex had ruined me; now I was horny as hell.

He stood in front of the stove, lazily stirring something. His hair was wet and loose around his shoulders, and his chest was bare again. All he had on was a clean pair of sweats.

Beck looked over his shoulder. His eyes grew hooded as they dragged down my figure, then made their way back up. "Come sit on the countertop."

My mind flashed back to the day before.

To the way we'd made out by the sink, and the way he'd had his mouth on me there.

My face flushed. "I'll help cook."

"Your feet are tired. Just sit down." He gestured me toward him, and I reluctantly crossed the room. When I saw him start to drop his spoon so he could lift me up, I slid onto the counter by myself.

I needed to avoid having his hands on any part of me.

It was hard enough to control myself when he *wasn't* touching me.

"Do you have something against shirts?" I asked.

"Do you have something against me being shirtless?" he countered.

He had me there.

"No. I would just be more... comfortable... if you wore a shirt."

Beck lifted an eyebrow at me. "My bare chest makes you uncomfortable?"

Yes.

In a horny, horny way.

I couldn't say that, though.

"It's distracting," I said instead.

"Ah." He kept stirring his food. "Well, your legs are distracting. And your neck. If I'm putting a shirt on, you need to cover up too."

"How can my *neck* be distracting?"

"Your neck is on the way to your chest. Have you already forgotten how much I like having you on my mouth?"

My body flushed hotter. "Okay, I'm leaving."

His hand landed on my thigh, holding me lightly in place. "I don't think you want me to chase you out right now, Si."

My gaze lowered to his erection, on clear display through his pants.

Hot damn.

"Tell me what you want in a mate," he said, distracting me.

My attention jerked up to the pan of chicken simmering in heavenly-smelling sauce. "Um... I don't really want a mate."

"It's too late for that. You *have* a mate. So, tell me what your ideal life with me would look like."

My face was still crazy hot. "I've never really thought about it. You tell me yours."

He nodded. "I'm not tied to any specific ideas in particular. Mainly, I've always wanted a companion. Someone to hold at night, and pull into my arms when life gets difficult. Someone to have fun with, and talk things out with."

My throat swelled a bit.

I liked the sound of that.

"Do you want to stay in Wildwood? And do you want kids?" I asked.

"I don't have any expectations. I assumed that when I met my mate, we'd figure out what was important to her and craft our life together around that."

"But what do you *want*?"

"If it was up to me, I'd like to stay in Wildwood permanently. I don't know that I *want* kids, but statistically, most mated couples eventually decide to have one or more after a few decades or centuries together."

My heart sank a little.

If I wasn't wrestling with the looming possibility of pregnancy, I would've loved his answer. Because I was, it wasn't what I wanted to hear.

"Do you want to stay in Wildwood, and have kids?" he asked me.

"I don't want to leave Wildwood. I feel safe here, for the first time in a long time. I've never thought about having kids, but when I was growing up, I was always alone. I promised myself that if I ever had kids, I would have a few, so they could have each other and wouldn't have to deal with that loneliness," I admitted.

"I like that. My siblings and I were close, before I lost them in the war. I'm the only one left now. My parents are still alive, though. They're already bugging me to meet you. The pack's gossip got back to them already."

"They live here?"

"Yes, they're both enforcers."

I lifted my eyebrows. "So they answer to you?"

He chuckled. "Yes. The relationship changes a lot over the course of eternity. It resembles friendship more than parenthood when you've been alive as long as I have."

That made sense, though it was bizarre to imagine. I hadn't been close with my parents even before social services took me from them for my safety when I was six. All I could really remember was their tempers, and the way their lives were controlled by their drug addictions. They weren't cruel to me, but they hadn't cared about me.

I would *definitely* never consider them my friends.

"This will be ready in a few minutes." Beck finally released my leg, stepping away from me so he could grab a few seasonings. He tasted the sauce with a finger, then added more, repeating the motion a few times.

I couldn't hide my smile at the way he cooked without a recipe. Baking didn't work like that, and if I made the attempt, my cookies would look and taste like shit.

He nodded when he was satisfied with it, and I watched him dish up two full plates. When he carried them to the table, I slipped off the countertop and grabbed silverware and water glasses.

I knew the food would be good before I even sat down.

SIENNA

WE ATE dinner in relative quiet, then cleaned up together before we sat down at the table with a deck of cards.

"What are we playing?" I asked as he shuffled.

"Strip poker."

My eyes narrowed.

He flashed me a grin that made my lower belly clench. "Loser doesn't strip their clothes—they have to be the first to share their thoughts about difficult subjects."

"What difficult subjects?"

He pulled a folded sheet of paper from his pocket and slid it across the table, finding a handwritten list.

-Sealing the bond

-Friends' opinions
-Wildwood Bitches
-Pack announcement
-Finances
-Work schedule
-Kids
-Sex
-Sleeping arrangements
-Communication
-Disagreements
-Goals
-Family
-Last Names
-Love languages
-Date nights
-Living arrangements
-Blood drinking

My eyes nearly bulged out when I looked at the list. "You want to talk about all of these?"

"Yep. Might as well get it over with. Things will be simpler when we're on the same page about everything."

I grimaced. "Alright."

I'd learned how to play *Texas Hold 'Em* with a few of the other ladies in the pack a few months earlier. It had been during one of my many evenings at the bar where I made small talk with the men the alphas were hoping would be my mate. We'd played a handful of times since, so Beck didn't have to explain the rules to me.

He set us both up with some poker chips, then dealt the cards. When he folded after the last card was shown, it was my turn to pick a topic that he would have to bring up first.

I scanned the list again quickly.

Which one sucked the least?

"Goals," I said.

He nodded. "My main goal right now is to win my mate's heart."

I rolled my eyes.

His lips curved. "While we settle things between us, I aim to set up a good security system on the house so I don't worry about you if you're home without me. Five years from now, my goal is to have a blissfully-happy mate, and a safe pack that functions smoothly."

"It already functions smoothly, doesn't it?"

"For the most part. It was much better when Wildwood wasn't at risk of being invaded by vampires, and we want to get it back to that again."

"You guys will never be safe while we're here," I said.

"Mated blood wolves are more hassle than they're worth to a vampire clan," Beck corrected. "When you're mated, they'll realize their efforts are a waste of time and leave us alone.

I didn't think it would be that simple, but didn't argue.

"What are your goals, Si?"

To find out whether or not I was expecting in two weeks.

To survive our mate bond without having sex again before my doctor's appointment, so I could avoid further risk of pregnancy.

Not to be a vampire's possession ever again.

"I don't really have any right now. I just want to make a lot of cookies," I said.

He chuckled, not looking surprised at all. "Alright."

With that, he handed the deck over. I shuffled and dealt, and soon enough, was pushing the chips in the center over to him after he destroyed me.

He didn't look at the list before picking a topic. "Let's talk about announcing our connection to the pack."

That was an easy one, at least.

"I don't care when or how we do it. It's entirely up to you," I said.

My words relaxed him a bit.

He admitted, "I'd like to announce our mating to the pack tomorrow. The longer we stay silent, the more people will gossip, and I'd prefer to avoid anyone following us around to take pictures of us."

I agreed, and that was that.

We played another hand, and I lost again.

"We already talked about kids," he said. "Are you okay with shelving the topic for about a year, and discussing it more thoroughly after we've had that time to settle and figure everything out?"

My stomach churned a little. "Sure."

In an ideal world?

Yes, absolutely.

That would be great.

But we weren't living in Ideal Nation.

Or at least, I wasn't.

And at some point, I'd need to tell Beck that he wasn't either.

Yikes.

We played another hand, and he crushed me yet again.

I sighed as he took my chips.

"Let's talk about the Wildwood Bitches group," he said.

"What about it?" I didn't even know why that was on the list, honestly. I only participated when someone asked me a direct question in the chat, and even then, I'd probably missed a few.

"I'd prefer if you make an announcement in there, too. I don't want them making you uncomfortable anymore."

Oh.

That.

"I wasn't really uncomfortable."

He gave me a look that said he didn't believe me.

And I *had* called him to ask if he was sleeping with anyone else because of that group chat. So, the doubt was valid.

"Alright, I can make an announcement there if anyone brings us up again in it after we've told the pack."

"That works."

We played another round.

I lost yet again.

"How about the living arrangements?" he asked me.

"I mean, you did abduct me," I pointed out.

"It seemed like a good call in the moment. If you'd rather I move into your house, I can make that work."

I blinked. "So we're definitely living together?"

"Yes."

"That's not up for debate?"

"Nope." He ran a hand through his hair, drawing my attention to his biceps.

I shook my head, forcing my attention back to his face. "It should be a conversation, at least."

"My wolf wouldn't let me sleep a room away from you. Half a neighborhood away would cost me my sanity. Functioning on less sleep would make it harder to control my instincts. My wolf would likely take over."

Oh.

"So we're living together, then."

He nodded.

I let out a short breath. "Your house is prettier, and I'm not attached to mine. Plus, my cat isn't a dick here. We'll stay."

"Good." The satisfaction in his eyes was thick. "You're off work tomorrow?"

"Yep."

"We'll move your things in the morning, so we have all day to get them organized."

"Alright." Though I agreed, I was starting to feel like I was losing every conversation he brought up. It was kind of irritating.

We played another round, though, and I finally won again.

Looking over the list, my lips curved downward.

I didn't want to talk about any of it.

"Family," I finally said.

"My parents want to meet you, like I was saying earlier. They want to have dinner together. You can decide when you're ready, but they'll probably be offended if we wait more than a week or so."

I grimaced. "Let's do it a week from now."

He agreed, and dealt another round of cards.

I lost again.

"Sleeping arrangements," he said.

"I'm not sharing a bed. If your wolf won't let you sleep in the other room, we can get bunkbeds or something." My voice was flat.

I had to put my foot down about something. The man was deciding everything.

And I wanted him badly enough that if we shared a bed, I'd probably roll over and climb on his cock during the night.

As much fun as that would be, I absolutely couldn't let it happen again until after my doctor's appointment, where I'd either go on birth control or find out there was no point in it.

He blinked. "I didn't think sharing a bed was that big of a deal. I could sleep in my wolf form if that would make you more comfortable."

"Nope. You take the floor or buy a bunk bed, or I'll sleep on the ground myself."

He studied me for a moment before he finally agreed. "I can push the spare mattress in."

"That works."

He was looking at me a little differently while we played the next round. Like he was curious.

But he still beat me.

And instead of picking one of the easier topics, like he had been, he said,

"Let's talk about sex."

My body tensed.

"That's not the reaction I hoped for," he remarked.

"I have no idea what you're talking about," I lied.

"You tensed. Your shoulders went tight. Your eyes hardened."

"Eyes can't *harden*."

"Yours did. Tell me why."

"Was that an order, Beckett?"

His gaze flashed, his lips curving upward. "Beckett, huh? You really don't want to talk about sex."

"It's not my preferred topic, no."

"Why not?"

I couldn't lie that it had been bad.

The man knew how good it had been for me. He'd legitimately *focused* on making it good for me.

"You fucked me without telling me what I was to you, knowing I'd walk away if you told me. It was manipulative. I don't want to talk about me being manipulated," I said.

His interest and amusement vanished instantly. "We didn't fuck, Sienna. We made love. And I wasn't manipulating you, I was getting to know you and showing you the benefits of having a mate."

"I'm sure you can see how it doesn't come off that way to me."

He dragged a hand through his hair. "I thought you would walk away if I told you what you were to me."

"I would've. And you probably would've chased me, like you did when I went to Tori's house."

"I definitely would've chased you. You're mine." There was an edge to his tone that made me hotter.

And despite what I was saying, I still wanted him. There was no doubt about that.

I still felt hurt.

I still hated that he'd kept the truth from me.

It just wouldn't stop me from sleeping with him again, if not for everything else.

"I can't take back what I did, so tell me how to make it right, Si."

"I wouldn't want you to take it back. I had fun, and you made me feel amazing. I'm just not ready to do it again. I'm not a spontaneous person. I'm not wild. You know I was a virgin before I was with you. I don't usually make decisions on the spur of a moment. I need space to figure things out. That's not too much to ask, is it?"

He shook his head.

He'd been following me long enough to be well aware of the way I eased into things.

Slowly, or not at all, if I could avoid it.

Which was exactly why he'd gone about things the way he had.

And I mean, it had worked. It had obviously worked.

I just wasn't ready to accept that.

"Alright. Space is understandable, given everything that happened. If you're living with me, and we're sleeping in the same room, we can stop right here and come back to everything else when you're ready. We don't need to figure it out right this second."

I swallowed roughly. "Thank you."

"I'd say it's the least I can do. Do you want to watch a movie instead?"

"Actually, I think I'm going to call it a night. I haven't had much sleep the last few days." I rubbed my eyes, hoping it would hide some of my overwhelming emotions.

He agreed without hesitation.

I watched him push the spare mattress into his bedroom, and after he grabbed a few extra blankets, we both curled up in our own beds in silence.

It was awkward.

I hated it.

But it was better than the alternative, so I just went to sleep.

WE WERE both quiet while we drove his truck to my place and packed everything the next morning.

During the short drive to his house, Beck kept glaring at my blood freezers in the rearview mirror.

I had to bite my lip to stop myself from smiling.

He was ridiculous, but it was kind of sweet.

Beck helped me organize my things in his house, then headed to the kitchen to make lunch. I had to follow him in, because I had cookies to make that couldn't wait another day. A few women in the pack were paying me to make them—one for a little girl's birthday party, and the other for a baby shower.

I had to make the cookies and frost some of them a few hours after they were done, so they had plenty of time to cool. There probably wouldn't be enough time to get to all of them in the morning, so I had to get going.

Music played in the kitchen while Beck cooked and I worked on my dough. He gave me the space I'd requested, and it wasn't nearly as awkward as it had been earlier.

We had lunch while my dough chilled, and the weirdness set back in for a few minutes. Madd called him before he was done eating, though, so he stepped out to talk to the alpha.

I stared down at my phone while I finished my food, contemplating whether or not I should smooth things over with Love.

While I was still hurt that she'd kept the secret, I felt bad for making her feel bad. That was probably a dumb thing to care about, but I *did* care about it.

After a few minutes, I decided to leave it alone for a few days. I finished my food and cleaned up the small mess from lunch, then went back to my cookies.

Beck came back in while I was rolling my dough. He frowned when he saw the kitchen. "You didn't need to clean up after me."

"You cooked," I pointed out.

"You're *still* cooking."

"Cleaning up after someone else cooks seems like basic courtesy. If we're going to live together, I think we can use some of that."

He let out a long breath that told me he was annoyed, but jerked his head in a nod. "Thank you."

"Mmhm."

I went back to my cookies, and his phone rang again.

It was slightly awkward... but it could've been worse, right?

BAUTHER

I FOUGHT like hell to give Sienna the space she wanted through the whole day. It was fucking painful.

By the time the pack run came around, I was grateful for an excuse to talk to her again, even if I had to try not to touch her more than necessary.

"We need to look like a team," I murmured to her, as we slipped out of the house. "The gossip will get worse if it doesn't seem like we're happy together."

She nodded, though her gaze was moving over the crowd of shifters on the street.

"Is it okay if I touch you tonight?"

"Yeah. If we want to sell it, we'll need to be really touchy. I'll do it too."

"Maybe we'll be able to breathe again when she's touching us," my wolf grumbled.

"You're going to get to run with her wolf soon enough, and I can't imagine she'll refuse to touch you."

"Fuck, I hope not."

I slipped my arm around her waist, easing her to my side so she wouldn't get bumped as we joined the crowd. There were dozens of curious eyes on us, but we ignored them.

Her scent was incredible, and my cock responded to it.

She wrapped her arm around my back, and I hardened even more.

I ached for her so much, it was driving me mad.

We made it to the place the pack always gathered before runs, and the crowd parted enough to let us through to the front. Madd and Love were already waiting up there, and Love immediately flashed Sienna a smile.

There was more to it than happiness. It looked like an apology.

Sienna reached over and squeezed her hand as we stepped into position beside them.

She leaned against me while Madd welcomed everyone, and while I announced our bond. She smiled when the pack cheered, and leaned in even closer, hugging me tighter.

It wasn't the naked, full-body hug I wanted, but it was a hell of an improvement from the way we'd spent the first part of the day.

I kept her body hidden from the pack's eyes while she stripped and shifted. Though I tried to keep my eyes from moving down her gorgeous bare back, I failed, and my gaze devoured her sexy figure.

Damn, I wanted her in a way I'd never wanted anything or anyone before.

The distance between us felt *wrong*.

I rubbed her wolf's head for a moment before I let mine out. He immediately rubbed his side against hers, burying his nose in her neck.

He inhaled her scent, growling, *"You smell perfect. Tell your human to stop hiding from mine. I need to smell you more."*

She let out a soft, laugh-like chuff. *"My human needs time to move on from the lies."*

"There were no lies. We never said you weren't our mate."

She rolled her eyes at him, and he stepped around to smell the other side of her. His chest rumbled at her smell.

The rest of the pack had already moved on and disappeared into the forest, but we clearly weren't in a hurry.

"Walk with me, mate," my wolf finally said, when he was content with how much they smelled like each other. *"Let me feel your side against mine."*

Her wolf chuffed again, still softly. She was almost a little bashful, too.

But they walked together until they were ready to run, then spent the rest of the night playing in the forest.

When we finally made it back home, we collapsed in our own separate beds—as much as I hated the distance—and crashed quickly.

SIENNA

BECK GAVE me space while I frosted my cookies all morning, and when early afternoon came around, he went with me to deliver them.

The ladies running the baby shower were full of gushy *thank you*'s, and the woman being celebrated teared up when she saw the blue and white bow-ties, diapers, and paw print cookies.

Beck was in a conversation with the woman's mate when I finished setting the cookies out, so I lingered in the kitchen a bit longer, acting like I was repositioning them so they looked better.

My eyes kept moving back to her, though.

The pregnant woman.

Her belly was insanely round, and the hand she had on her lower back told me it was probably aching. Her hair was messy, and she looked tired, too, but there was something in her eyes.

Light?

Excitement?

It was hard to read.

I couldn't look away.

Two of the women running the shower struck up a conversation to my left, and I couldn't help but overhear it.

"Every time I go to one of these, I want to have another one. I wish pregnancy wasn't such a bitch," one of the women said.

My lips curved upward slightly at her candor. I'd never been a part of a conversation about pregnancy before, and I was curious.

"It's hellish," the other woman agreed. "But those cute little furballs are worth the pain. They drive me insane when I'm with them—but as soon as I leave the house, I miss them."

"I know, it's so stupid!" the first exclaimed. "How can something so infuriating be so adorable? And all the sticky, sweet kisses... it's not fair. My mate needs to be smaller and cuter, so I stop wanting more babies."

Both of them laughed, and I bit my lip to stop myself from doing the same.

I could no longer keep moving cookies around without seeming like a weirdo, so I let myself look at the pregnant woman one more time before I slipped back to Beck's side. He wrapped his arm around me absentmindedly, pulling me closer as he wrapped up the conversation. A few minutes later, he walked me back to his truck, where the rest of the cookies were boxed up for transport.

We didn't say anything on the ride to the house where the birthday party would be.

My mind was still on the pregnant woman.

And the possibility that I could be in her shoes in a handful of months.

When we got to the next house, the three-year old girl was running around in a pink dress, with a tutu tied around her waist and a crown on her head. She was chasing an older girl around the house, both of them carrying sparkly wands and yelling something about a queen.

"Thank you so much," the girls' mom gushed, as Beck carried the cookie boxes over to the trays she'd set out for them.

I'd met her a handful of times, so we knew each other vaguely, though I'd never met her kids. One of which was in her arms—a baby boy I knew was only a few months old.

One of the little girls in the other room started screaming, and Ellen sighed. "Would you mind taking him for a minute? I need to put an end to the drama before any of the guests arrive."

Without waiting for an answer, she set her baby in my arms.

I couldn't stop myself from going still. Very, very still.

I'd never held a baby before.

He was so small and light.

And the way those adorable blue eyes stared up at me while his binky bounced up and down lightly in his mouth was mesmerizing.

He was so perfect, my chest ached a little.

Or maybe a lot.

"Hello," I said softly, not sure what else to say to him.

Beck stepped back up to my side. "How's Elliot today?" He leaned over my shoulder, tickling the little guy on the belly while grinning down at him. "Aren't you handsome?"

My chest tightened more.

A lot more.

Elliot gave Beck a gummy grin back, and I swear, my heart stopped.

The other ladies were right.

Babies were insanely adorable. *Irresistibly* adorable.

Maybe it wouldn't be so bad if I was pregnant, after all.

Maybe I would like being a mom.

Beck cooed at the little guy, and I couldn't stop myself from joining in. Though I felt weird about it at first, when he started giving us that gummy grin, the weirdness faded quickly.

He was gorgeous.

Absolutely gorgeous.

When Elliot's dad came over and scooped him out of my arms, thanking us for helping out, the ache in my chest returned.

I hadn't wanted to let him go.

Maybe I wanted a baby of my own to love and take care of. It obviously wouldn't always be as easy as holding them and smiling at them—but I'd been through some really difficult shit, and I'd survived just fine.

So why couldn't I survive motherhood?

Beck didn't bring up the baby as we got in his truck again, or as we drove home, but me?

I couldn't stop thinking about him.

Or about the appointment that was still a long thirteen days away.

I WENT BACK to work the next morning, and Beck went back to protecting me. Love apologized again while she, Tori, and I worked together, and I decided to forgive her for keeping the truth from me.

She'd been in a hard position, with her only options being to betray Madd and Beck, or to keep the secret from me. If she'd known much longer, I felt like she probably would've given in and told me, so it was alright.

We moved on, and that was that.

Both girls kept my secret, thankfully.

The days passed by slowly as I got closer and closer to the appointment. I could tell Beck hated giving me space, but he was doing it anyway, which I appreciated.

I met his family like we planned, and it was a little awkward, but they were really nice.

When the appointment finally arrived, my best friends and I enacted a plan we'd cooked up. All three of us had picked up a shift for that day.

They joined me at my workstation—which was in Beck's line of sight—and I slipped out of view when he wasn't looking. Tori and Love would cover for me if he asked where I was, and the office wasn't far from the bakery, so I wouldn't be gone long.

Hopefully, he wouldn't realize I'd left at all.

My heart beat rapidly as I pulled away from the bakery, my lips stretching in a wide but reluctant smile as I put more and more distance between me and Beck.

Eventually, I'd have to come clean to him about the whole situation.

Soon, probably.

He'd been nothing but respectful since the night we'd played poker, so I owed him the truth after I figured it out myself.

When I slipped into the waiting room, a few curious gazes landed on me.

I recognized all three of the women immediately. They were all pack members.

Which didn't bode well for me, or for secrecy.

Guess I was going to have to tell Beck sooner, rather than later.

Like, immediately.

Fantastic.

The receptionist was also in the pack, and recognized me instantly. She took me to a room immediately, hiding me away from the prying eyes in the waiting area, but the damage was already done.

Maybe I'd get lucky, and they'd just circulate rumors about me getting a yearly woman's exam or something.

The doctor came in a few minutes later. She was calm and happy, and took my blood and other measurements herself. She told me she could get the results within the hour if I waited, so I waited.

A message came through ten minutes into waiting.

TORI

Bauther's onto us

LOVE

He has murder in his eyes

TORI

Shut off your phone if you don't want to get bombarded with calls and texts from him. Been there, done that, kinda sucks

I let out a long breath.

Telling him after the appointment would be the easiest, and the most logical. But if he'd realized I was gone, he was going to freak out, and I felt too bad to put him through that.

So, I texted them back.

ME

I'll handle it. Thanks ladies

They sent hearts and kiss emojis, and I pulled up Beck's contact, sending him the address for the building I was in.

ME

I'm at the doctor's office. I know this isn't the best way to tell you, but I wasn't on birth control when I went home from the bar with you.

A bubble popped up for a long moment, then disappeared, like he was typing a message but changed his mind.

I watched, waiting for the message to come through or for more bubbles, but none came.

Letting out a long breath, I set my phone on my leg and looked at the clock.

Only thirty-five minutes to go.

Five more minutes passed painfully slowly, before the door to the room I was in swung open. "She's right in here," a pleasant female voice said.

Beck strode in, his face calm but his eyes storming. He didn't so much as look at the woman as he closed the door behind us.

And locked it.

I bit my lip, my heartbeat skyrocketing.

He crouched in front of my chair, those intense eyes catching mine and holding my gaze as he set his hands on my knees. "Tell me everything."

Right.

Everything was probably a good place to start.

"I didn't think about birth control," I said quietly. "It didn't even cross my mind until after I got home that night, and saw a text in the Wildwood Bitches group about how adorable our kids would be. I panicked and called Love. Neither of us knew anything about werewolf fertility. The vampires didn't teach us any of that, and unlike my best friends, I got my IUD out when I got away from the clan. It felt like taking control of my life again, for some ridiculous reason."

I continued, "Madd told us that werewolves are crazy fertile with their mates. I said it was a good thing we weren't mates, but they both went quiet for a minute. Then, Love told me to dig out your blood bag, and call her back afterward. I did, and realized what you were to me."

"I didn't know what to do. She'd kept the truth from me, so staying didn't feel safe, and you'd lied to me—so I went to Tori's place, where you found me. I called the doctor the next day, and she said I had to wait two weeks before a blood test could give me an answer." I gestured toward the tape wrapped around the inside of my elbow, holding cotton over the place the needle had stabbed me.

Beck took a long breath in, then let it out.

He closed his eyes.

The veins in his neck were bulging. The ones in his forehead, too.

I resisted the urge to shrink away. Even at his angriest, he couldn't hurt me. His wolf would never allow it.

"And you didn't tell me until now, because?" he finally asked, his voice strained.

"Because I didn't want to see your reaction until I found out myself. If I'm pregnant, I'm having this baby whether you like it or not. I'll raise it myself. Love and Tori will help when I get overwhelmed. I'll learn self-defense to keep him or her safe, and—"

His hands cupped my face roughly, his eyes bright and angry. "If there's a baby, it's mine just as much as it's yours, and I will love the fuck out of it. I'll be the best fucking dad you've ever seen. Both of you will be mine to protect, and that's all there is to it. I care a fucking lot about you, Si, whether you're ready to accept it or not."

I let out a breath. "That was a lot of fucks."

"All of them." He kissed me hard on the lips, then released my face.

After he unlocked the door, he stepped back over to me and scooped me up out of the chair—then sat back down with me on his lap.

"The doctor might feel weird if she comes in here and sees me sitting on you," I said, though his body felt incredible against my back.

He wrapped his arms around my waist, holding me where I was. "Then she should've provided two chairs."

Sure enough, there was only the one chair and the examination table. "I can sit on the—"

"No." Beck didn't even debate it for a second. Or loosen his hold on me. "I'm not letting go of you right now. And we're going home to play poker again as soon as this is over, whether you like it or not."

My body flushed at the dominance in his voice.

His definition of playing poker was *having difficult conversations*. I didn't think I'd be able to avoid those topics any longer.

Even if I could, I was realizing that I shouldn't.

"Are you asking me on a date?"

"Yes. For the rest of our lives, actually. Now, do you want me to distract you with a conversation while we wait for the results, or do you just want me to hold you?"

The question made my throat swell. "Just hold me, please."

Beck adjusted his arms, so they held me securely as I leaned back against him. He rested his chin on the top of my head, and we waited.

And waited.

And waited.

His thumbs stroked slow, soft shapes where they rested on my skin.

And finally, the doctor came back in. To her credit, she wasn't caught off-guard in the slightest when she found me sitting on Beck's lap.

"Beta." She dipped her head toward him quickly before her gaze met mine. "Sienna, are you comfortable sharing the results of the test with him?"

Her leaving it up to me, despite his place in the pack, made me feel important. Respected, too.

"Yes. He deserves to know," I said.

He pressed lightly into my skin, thanking me.

Her lips lifted in a small smile, and she handed me a sheet of paper. "Then let me be the first to congratulate you both."

I looked down at the paper she'd handed me.

There were numbers on it, but I didn't look at the numbers.

My eyes went to the words.

Positive.

Pregnant.

I sucked in a breath.

Beck's fingers pressed deeper into my hips.

She gave us a folder with more information, as well as an estimated due date, then sent us on our way.

We were both quiet on our way to the parking lot. My car was there, but I didn't protest as he walked me to his truck and helped me into the passenger seat.

Instead of walking away when I was sitting down, he wrapped his arms around me and hugged me, tightly. My eyes stung as I squeezed him back, holding on for dear life.

I wasn't upset.

I didn't wish we'd gotten a different answer.

But... I was a little overwhelmed.

"July 10th," he murmured into my hair.

My eyes stung more. "It's going to be a big change."

"It's probably too soon to admit this, but I'm excited, Si. So fucking excited."

I laughed, though I choked on my emotions when I did. "I'm getting there."

Beck chuckled, his body strong and steady against mine.

He released me, taking his seat and pulling out of the parking lot. One of his hands caught mine, slipping between my fingers while he steered with the other. "I'm sorry you had to handle the stress on your own for the past few weeks, and I hope you haven't been blaming yourself. I'm equally at fault here. I should've asked if you were on birth control, or used a damn condom."

"You were excited that you found me. I was excited to have sex. Neither of us thought it through," I admitted. "Tori and Love have been here to talk to me. I wanted to tell you... but I didn't want to screw things up. And I kind of wanted revenge, if I'm being completely honest."

"I deserved it. Now, can we agree that there will be no more secrets from here on out?"

"No more secrets," I agreed.

And as we drove through the city, it felt like a weight had been lifted from my shoulders.

We would figure the baby thing out together.

We would figure *everything* out together.

Because like it or not, from there on out, we had to become a team.

thirteen

SIENNA

WE PICKED up lunch on the way home, and after we ate, sat down with our cards and poker chips.

Beck wrote out a new list. It was the old list, minus a few topics we'd already dealt with, plus a few new ones.

He handed it to me, and dealt the cards while I looked over it.

-Sealing the bond
-Friends' opinions
-Finances
-Work schedule
-Sex
-Sleeping arrangements
-Communication
-Disagreements

-Last Names
-Love Languages
-Date nights
-Blood drinking
-Childcare
-Parenting

I'd dreaded all of the topics the last time we sat down to discuss them, but now... I was kind of excited. Without the secrets hanging between us, and with the time that had passed, I actually wanted to figure things out with him.

Of course, I hadn't processed the fact that I was pregnant. That one would take some time to wrap my mind around, but we'd get there.

We played through the first hand, and unsurprisingly, I lost.

I sighed dramatically, though I really wasn't disappointed.

"Let's talk about sealing the bond," Beck said.

"Alright. I don't feel strongly about it, but I know it's important to you to solidify everything between us. It would probably make me safer, too, so I think it's a good idea."

He nodded. "I would prefer we seal it as soon as possible. It offers you protection, in a way nothing except drinking my blood can."

I bit my lip at the mention of drinking his blood.

His curved upward.

Something told me *that* conversation was going to make my toes curl.

Beck shuffled and dealt again, and we played through another hand.

"Are you cheating?" I asked, when he won again.

He laughed. "No. I haven't played this enough to know how to cheat."

"There goes my excuse for sucking at it."

He glanced at the list briefly. "How about communication and disagreements?"

"Communication is pretty important. Disagreements make me feel stressed. I don't know what there really is to talk about them."

"I'd like us to have a plan for how and when we communicate. It doesn't sound romantic to schedule a time, but if we tell each other about our day while we cook dinner every night, it keeps us talking. And having a plan for disagreements can help keep them manageable, in the same way."

My mind went back to something my friends had mentioned. "Love told me her and Madd take baths together, and talk through things there."

Beck grinned. "A bathtub would be a good place to disagree. It'd be hard to be angry at each other while we're naked."

"Alright, then we'll fight in the tub. And I like the idea of talking every day. Maybe we plan on talking at night, when we go to bed? Because sometimes, we'll do dinner with the pack or our friends."

He agreed, then shuffled again.

My losing streak continued, and he flashed me an apologetic smile. "Our last topic leads right into sleeping arrangements, Si."

"You want to share a bed, right?" I checked.

He wouldn't have put it back on the list if he was satisfied with the current arrangements.

"Unless it will still make you uncomfortable, yes."

"If we're being honest, I only didn't want to share a bed because I was afraid I would accidentally have sex with you again before my doctor's appointment," I admitted.

He laughed, loudly. "You probably would've."

"It's likely." I brushed a few strands of hair out of my eyes. "I'm on board with sleeping together."

His eyes gleamed.

"Sharing a bed," I edited.

The wickedness in his gaze didn't fade, but he didn't push me any harder.

There would be more opportunities for that when we got to the later topics on the list.

He dealt again, and I lost.

Again.

He brought up love languages, which I'd never heard of. After he gave me a rundown of the languages being the biggest ways we show love, our game paused for a few minutes while I took an online test.

Soon enough, I'd learned that my main love language was quality time. His was tied between acts of service and physical touch, which didn't surprise me in the slightest.

After another round of losing, in which we agreed to do a date night one day every week, I finally won a round.

I scanned the remaining items on the list.

-Friends' opinions
-Finances
-Work schedule
-Sex
-Last Names
-Date nights
-Blood drinking
-Childcare
-Parenting

Sheesh.

Most of them were difficult.

"Let's do the friends' opinion one, because I have no idea what it's about," I said.

He dipped his head. "Love and Tori mentioned that they didn't think you and I were compatible. I was hoping we could talk about it."

I blinked.

Damn.

I didn't know he'd heard that.

"They should never have said that, and I wasn't a part of the conversations when they did. They only brought it up to me once or twice. Apparently, they thought you were too dominant for me, and not nice enough, which is dumb. You're dominant, sure, but you don't try to dominate *me*. And you're always nice to me."

"It doesn't bother me that they were looking out for you; I just want us to be open about discussing when someone talks negatively about us to each other. In my mind, a mated pair functions as one. If someone insults you, they've insulted me, and I'll deal with it."

"So I need to stand up for you too," I finished.

"You don't *have* to," he started, but I cut him off.

"If we're going to be a team, we're doing it right. I'll shut Tori and Love down if they say anything bad about you again. For the record, they haven't said anything bad since you abducted me."

"Thank you." He reached for my hand across the table, and squeezed it lightly. "I appreciate that."

"You're a good guy, Beck. Things have been messy since we found out about us, but we're figuring it out."

He lifted my hand to his lips, and kissed my knuckles lightly.

When he won the next round, he studied the list the same way I had.

"Let's do last names," he finally said.

"I'm not attached to my last name, and I grew up human, so if we're going to be mated, I'd like to take yours," I said. "I don't want a different last name than our baby."

The satisfaction in his eyes at my words made me smile.

I lost the next hand too, and he picked another topic.

"Work schedules and finances."

"Why do these need to be combined?" I checked.

"Because the amount of money we have and need should affect how much we work, shouldn't it?"

Right.

"Well, I don't love my job at the bakery," I admitted. "I've been slowly growing my cookie-decorating business. In an ideal world, I would decorate cookies full-time so I can stay home and work here. I don't make enough money from the cookies to pull that off, though, and I don't like charging people too much. The pack pays you, right?"

"Yes. I was working as a firefighter two days a week before we found out you and Love were in town. Since then, I've been running the pack's security full-time. I make enough money and have enough saved that we could both stop working entirely and live comfortable lives for the next few hundred years."

Hot damn.

"I'd like to combine our finances," he added. "If it makes you more comfortable to keep your own account separate from mine, that's fine. We'll transfer money into it, and you can use it as a security blanket that I have no access to. But, I've already added your name to my account. Your cards are in my wallet. I was trying to figure out a way to give them to you without pissing you off."

I shook my head, unable to hide my smile. "I should've expected that."

"Yep." He lifted my hand to his lips, kissing my knuckles lightly again. "You will always be taken care of, Si. Always. Whether or not you quit your job is entirely up to you, but I'd like to have the freedom to spend a lot of time together. And with more days off, you could focus on growing your business if that's what you want."

My heart soared. "I'll take a few days to think about it, but I'll probably quit and focus on the cookies."

He smiled.

We played another round, and I lost again.

I would've been more surprised if I won, at that point.

"Let's talk about parenting and childcare. We don't need to figure out any details or make any decisions, obviously, but I want to have an idea of your thoughts on them so I don't start making plans that you'll hate."

That was actually pretty damn reasonable.

"Okay. I have some terrible memories of being in foster homes when I was a kid, so I'll probably have a hard time trusting anyone else. I'm sure we could find a good childcare or nanny or something if we tried, but I would rather we take care of the baby together. If money's not an issue, I can do most of that myself, and cut back on my work if necessary. As far as parenting goes, I have no idea how to be a parent. I'll have to read some books or something."

Beck nodded. "We'll both read books. And I'm definitely on board with taking care of the baby together; I think it's fair if we split the time and effort, so I still have enough time with the pack and you still have the time you need for your business."

"That sounds perfect." My lips tilted upward.

Beck's did too.

He shuffled, and dealt again.

I looked down at the list, and my smile morphed into a grimace.

-Sex
-Blood drinking

We'd reached the most intense subjects on the damn list.

We played through the round, and unsurprisingly, I lost.

I heaved a sigh. "I don't want to talk about either of these things."

Beck chuckled. "You could always strip."

My eyebrows lifted.

"It *is* strip poker. You've got at least a few items of clothing you could rid yourself of before you have to tell me anything else."

He was on to something.

Stripping would buy myself time... and it would change the mood.

My body warmed a bit at the thought.

There was no reason we couldn't have sex, since we'd gotten through the doctor's appointment. It wasn't like he could knock me up *again*.

I'd forgiven him for keeping the truth from me, so that wasn't in the way, either.

"Alright, I'm paying with my sweater," I decided, tugging it over my head and dropping it on the ground.

Beck's chest rumbled in satisfaction as his gaze moved over my lace bra. "Good choice."

After he'd looked his fill, he dealt another hand.

Which I lost.

I slipped my pants off, and his chest rumbled again, louder.

"You hard yet?" I asked him, as I sat back down. The wooden chair was warm against my mostly-bare ass, and I was definitely getting wet between my thighs thanks to the way he was looking at me.

"As a fucking rock."

I didn't try to hide my smile.

He dealt again, and finally lost.

My smile widened.

He didn't say a word as he peeled his shirt off.

My body flushed, my eyes moving slowly over his torso.

Damn, he was beautiful.

I wanted to touch him, badly.

We played again, and I lost.

My eyes were locked with Beck's as I reached behind my back and undid the clasp of my bra.

And as I slid the straps down my arms.

And dropped the fabric on the floor.

His gaze was hot. "I don't have anything on under my pants. If you lose the next one, the game's over, and you sit on my lap."

"What if *you* lose?"

"I kneel under the table and spend the next hour fucking you with my tongue."

Ohh.

Damn.

"Alright. You can't fold without looking at the cards, though. We have to play the round through, and leave it up to luck."

His eyes were wicked. "Deal."

He took the cards, and I held my breath while he dealt them.

I didn't even care whether I won or lost.

Sitting on him, which would undoubtedly lead to having sex, or letting him eat me out?

Both would be a victory in my books.

We flipped the cards one by one, not bothering with making bets. When the last one was showing, I set mine down.

"A pair of fours," I said. It wasn't great, but it was better than nothing.

He set his down too. "Pair of aces."

He'd won.

I stood slowly, my lips curving upward. "Damn."

"Bummer," he agreed, not bothering to hide the heat in his gaze as they moved over me. "Pay up, Si."

I'd never been more excited to pay someone in my life.

fourteen

SIENNA

I SLID my thong down my legs slowly, then stepped out of it and walked around the table.

Beck moved his chair back a few inches, so there was plenty of room for me.

"You're gorgeous." His voice was low as he watched me move, and his hands caught the backs of my thighs as soon as I started to straddle him.

I lowered myself down over his cock, the length of him hard against my clit. "Ohh, you feel good."

I rocked my hips a little, and he groaned. "I've missed you."

"Me too. Have you touched yourself?"

"Jerked off in the shower every fucking day, with a picture of your perfect body in my mind." He dragged his hands up my chest and took my breasts, dragging his thumbs over my nipples. "These tits... I'd kill for them. Have you touched yourself?"

"I was too scared you'd hear," I admitted. "I tried once, and couldn't keep myself quiet enough."

He gave me a gravelly chuckle. "Good. I don't want you quiet, Si."

I didn't want me quiet either.

He continued working my nipples, making my hips rock more. "We need to talk about sex."

"What about it?"

"I want to have it. A lot of it. Any time either of us is horny."

"Sounds like fun."

His lips captured mine, and I slid my tongue into his mouth without pause. He squeezed my breasts hard, and I rocked against him.

As our tongues tangled, my need grew hot and fierce. I pulled away just long enough to breathe, "I need you inside me."

His chest rumbled against mine. "It's been too long. You need my fingers first, or it's going to hurt."

"I'm tougher than I look."

"I'm not hurting you, Si. The last time we were together was your first."

"And second, and third, and fourth."

"If you want my cock, you take my fingers," he growled. "End of the damn discussion."

"I thought I was in charge," I tossed back.

His mouth crashed into mine, and he kissed me harder. Rougher.

I pulled away after a moment. "*Beckett*. Tell me I'm in charge."

"You're in charge," he gritted out.

"Give me your cock, *now*."

He growled, but lifted me off his lap long enough to shove his pants out of the way.

When he lowered me back down, the head of his cock pressed against my entrance, and I moaned.

His fingers met my clit. "Slow, Si. Take me *slow*, or it's going to hurt."

"Alright." I lowered myself over him, and we groaned together when his tip finally entered me.

It *was* tight.

But he was wrong about it hurting. He felt incredible inside me.

I gave my body a second to adjust before I sank down further.

And further.

I was gasping for breath when he finally bottomed out.

One of his hands gripped my breast. The other had the top of my thigh, his thumb pressed against my clit.

"You feel so good," I said, moving my hips just a little to drag myself closer to the edge as I got used to the feel of him inside me. The way he worked my clit while he filled me was insane. "So, so good."

"You're fucking surreal," he gritted out. "This one's going to be quick. We'll take our time the second round."

"Agreed."

I swiveled my hips more.

He pressed hard against my clit, and I lost it.

My cries echoed through the room as I shattered on his cock, riding him hard. He snarled, losing control with me.

I dropped my head to his shoulder, panting through my pleasure. His chin landed on my head, his arms wrapped around me and holding me securely to his chest.

"Damn, I love the way you feel," he said into my hair.

I couldn't stop the stupid smile that curved my lips.

Or the warmth in my chest.

He stood up without letting go of me, and carried me into our room. "Careful, Sprinkles is on the bed."

"I hate that cat," I grumbled, and he laughed.

When we reached the bed—the actual one, not the mattress on the floor in the other corner—Beck lowered us both to the surface, with his body below mine. We were still intertwined, and neither of us had any desire to change that.

"We still have to talk about you feeding from me, Si," he said, brushing a few loose strands of hair out of my eyes. His hair was still tied up, and I hadn't gotten around to tugging it free yet.

"I know I have to drink your blood. There's no way around that. I'm just nervous, because I've never bitten anyone before. Drinking from the vein sounds intimate."

"And this isn't intimate?" His voice was playful, and his gaze made it clear he was just teasing me.

"It is, which is why I was nervous about sex, too. But as addictive as sex is, it's not anywhere near as binding as blood drinking."

"Until there's a baby involved."

"That's a very valid point."

Beck chuckled, brushing his fingers through my hair again.

"Tell me all the reasons I should bite you," I said, staring down at him.

His lips curved upward. "My blood was made for you. It'll taste fucking incredible, and it'll make the sex even better, from what I've heard."

"I've heard that too."

"On top of that, drinking my blood will trap me to you."

"And *me* to *you*," I countered.

"Mates live and die together. If you go, I go too. If you starve, we'll starve together. I'll have to feed you to keep us both alive, so drinking from me guarantees that I'll always be here."

It was a good selling point.

A very good selling point.

"Alright, I'll do it," I said.

"Try not to sound so excited, Si."

I smiled. "I'll come around."

"You'll definitely *come*."

I laughed. "I don't doubt that."

Beck grinned. "I missed hanging out with you like this. It was a long two weeks."

"It was. Let's not do it again."

"Agreed." He brushed his fingers through my hair, then glanced over at Sprinkles. I'd forgotten she was there until my gaze followed his over to her.

"You should try to move her," I said. "She hates me."

"She doesn't hate you."

"She definitely does."

He reached over and hooked an arm lightly over her torso, pulling her across the bed. I made a noise of protest, but cut myself off when she licked his arm, then rubbed her head up against it.

When he tugged her closer to me, she rubbed her head and arm against my side...

And purred.

My eyes widened.

"She never hated you, she just hated your house and had no other way to communicate that. It probably smelled bad. A handful of other shifters lived there before you."

Well, I hadn't considered that.

Even if I had, it wouldn't have changed anything. It wasn't like I could move before. The pack gave me free housing, and my job at the bakery didn't pay enough to afford the price of housing in Wildwood on my own.

She licked my arm, and my lips curved upward.

"Maybe Sprinkles isn't so bad," my wolf murmured.

"I guess she just needed to feel safe."

We spent a few minutes petting her lightly before she jumped down to the floor and slipped out of the room, leaving us alone.

"She should've been like that when I adopted her to keep me company," I remarked.

"Then you wouldn't have needed me." He tickled my side, and I wiggled a bit. The motion made his cock throb inside me, and my hips moved lightly in response.

One of his hands slid down to my ass. The other cupped my face, tilting my head back. His lips met mine softly.

Gently.

Sweetly.

I kissed him back, my tongue moving slowly with his.

It was warm.

Intimate.

Everything.

We moved together as we kissed, the flames of desire burning between us.

His lips finally trailed down my throat and over my shoulder, and he murmured, "Bite me, Si."

I was too lost to my lust to protest.

Even if I hadn't been, I knew it was inevitable. I needed his blood in my veins.

My fangs were already descended when my lips pressed to the side of his neck.

My teeth pierced his skin, and his taste filled my mouth.

Sweet.

Spicy.

Hot.

Perfect.

He tasted *perfect.*

With one motion, Beck rolled us over. My back met the mattress, and he thrust into me harder.

Faster.

Rougher.

My venom was stealing his control, tuning him into his basest needs and desires.

I moaned against his skin as he drove into me again, and again, taking me over the edge of my pleasure.

Feeding from him was bliss.

Absolute bliss.

I never wanted it to end.

He roared with his climax, filling me with his release.

I cried out, my fangs sliding free of his skin as I shattered once more.

We were both breathing hard when we came down from the high. The weight of Beck's body pressed against mine, comfortable in a way I never would've expected.

"You're incredible." His lips brushed my forehead, and he squeezed my ass lightly. "How is feeding from the vein?"

"Never drinking from a bag again," I mumbled.

He chucked, rumbling against me. "Glad we're on the same page."

"Definitely."

Beck rolled over, pulling me on top of him and tugging the blanket over our bodies. "How are you feeling?"

"Tired. A nap sounds really good."

"Then let's nap." He kissed my head again. "I'm never letting you go, Si. I hope you know that."

"I'm getting there."

His hand slid over the curve of my ass slowly.

"That feels amazing," I murmured.

"Good. Sleep well." He kissed my head yet again, and I fell asleep with the low rumble of his voice playing on repeat in my ears.

THE SOUND of our doorbell ripped me out of sleep. My face stung after I yanked it off Beck's chest, my mind disoriented from the sudden interruption.

"I'll get it," he said, smoothing his hand over my ass again. I got the impression he hadn't been asleep, and his eyes were warm as they moved over my face.

It rang again when he didn't move immediately.

"It's probably my friends," I said, rubbing my eyes with the back of my hand. "I forgot to text them after the appointment."

"I'll send them home." He set me on the mattress and slipped out of bed, grabbing a pair of sweats from the dresser before he headed out.

I knew he wasn't going to be able to get rid of them, so I rolled to my feet, stumbling to his closet. One of his shirts would cover enough skin for a conversation with Love and Tori.

Beck opened the door while I tugged it over my head, and my lips curved upward when I heard a demanding,

"Where is she?"

I pulled it into place and made my way out.

"Hey," I called, padding up behind Beck. Luckily, I'd made it before they started threatening him.

"You were supposed to call us!" Love exclaimed.

"We're dying here," Tori added.

I slipped between my mate and my friends, and his arms slid around my waist.

Love's and Tori's eyes both followed his arms, widening before they lifted back to mine. They knew I'd been avoiding anything that would lead to any sort of physical contact with him.

"I'm pregnant," I said.

The words sounded insane when I said them aloud.

Their eyes widened further, even though we'd all known that was pretty likely to be the case.

"Due in July," Beck added, his arms tightening around my middle.

"Are we happy about this?" Tori asked me, her gaze meeting mine.

I nodded, not bothering to fight my small smile. "We're happy about it."

Grins stretched across my friends' faces. They both surged forward, throwing their arms around me and Beck. I didn't like them touching him while he wasn't wearing a shirt, but figured they were used to being around gigantic, muscular male wolves.

Plus, they were both permanently mated.

"Congrats!" Love exclaimed. "We're happy for you!"

"And glad you seemed to have worked out *other things*, too," Tori teased, as they released us.

I laughed.

She was talking about sex.

And we had definitely figured it out, so she wasn't wrong.

"Thankfully, yes," Beck agreed.

Tori and Love grinned wider.

I rolled my eyes, but my smile didn't go anywhere.

"We'll leave you to it," Love said, still grinning. "After you've had a few days to settle, we want to get together for dinner at my house. Madd said he'll cook steak for everyone."

I'd heard a dozen times from her how good her mate was at cooking steak, so I was excited to try it. "Alright."

"I'd like it to be known that I call dibs on being the baby's godmother," Tori added, as Love tugged her down the driveway to give us space. "And you should name it after me!"

Beck chuckled as he pulled the door shut, his arm still wrapped around my waist.

"Where were we?" he murmured, pulling me back into the house and capturing my lips again.

I smiled, and kissed him back without missing a beat.

SIENNA

WE SPENT the next few days talking.

Laughing.

Trading stories.

Enjoying the pack's gossip.

Playing *actual* strip poker.

Getting to know each other's bodies.

By the time we finally made it to Love's house for dinner, I was all-in with Beck. We hadn't sealed our bond yet, but it was only a matter of time.

After Love let us in, Beck left me at the door with a kiss. He carried our sheet of veggie kebabs into the kitchen, joining Madd and Vex as they cooked. The kebabs would go on the grill soon, but the guys were handling it.

Love and Tori threw their arms around me, pulling me in for a group hug. I hugged them back, my smile wide and happy.

"Mating looks good on you," Love teased.

"It looks good on all of us," Tori said, her own lips stretched in a grin. Her eyes dipped to my arms—and widened when she saw the box of sugar cookies I was holding. "Damn, you're the best."

We ate, talked, and played cards until midnight came around. Then, Beck dragged me back to our house and made love to me.

Slowly.

Sweetly.

Blissfully.

When we were done, I cuddled up against him. His arms were around me, holding me close.

"I think I'm in love with you, Beck," I whispered, voicing the words that had been running through my mind.

It was too soon.

Everything had happened too fast.

But I wouldn't have traded it for anything.

"I'm in love with you too, Si. And I always will be. *Aeternum.*"

Aeternum was the word to ignite a mate bond.

It meant *forever*, and sealed two souls just as long.

I didn't have to reply.

I knew I could've stayed quiet.

Beck would've waited as long as I needed him to, despite our conversation about sealing the bond soon.

But I didn't *want* to wait.

I wanted him to know that I cared about him just as much as he cared about me.

"*Aeternum*," I murmured back.

For a moment, time stood still.

Tingles ran down my spine and through my body.

I felt as something within me changed, falling into place when our bond sealed our souls as one.

We were far from perfect, but we were together.

We were committed.

And I couldn't wait to see what our future would hold.

epilogue

BAUTHER

OUR THREE-YEAR-OLD RAN around the house with Tori and Vex while Sienna bit into a croissant. She was leaning up against me, using her rounded belly as a table to hold the sugar cookie she was going to have for dessert.

"I can't wait to be as far along as you so I have a built-in table," Love complained, her hand resting on her own small baby bump. "All I have right now is gas."

"Gas is way better than the tiny punk kicking you in the ribs. I'd take gas over a table any day," Sienna said.

Both her pregnancies had gone smoothly, which was a damn miracle. I would've felt like shit if she'd struggled after I accidentally knocked her up.

"Dad!" our toddler yelled, sprinting toward me. He was a handful—one I was grateful for every fucking day.

I caught him smoothly, careful not to bump my mate's belly.

"Sorry. I think we might've riled him up a little too much," Tori laughed, breathless from chasing the little guy around.

"No worries," Sienna smiled, as our little man told me excitedly about everything he'd been doing with his Aunt Tori and Uncle Vex.

"How's our peanut doing in there today?" Tori asked, plopping down next to Love. Madd was on her other side, but he didn't say anything as Tori touched Love's belly.

"He's actually a grapefruit today," Love said.

"Aww, I can't wait to be the cool aunt again." She rubbed her hand lightly on Love's belly, then did the same to Sienna's.

I brushed a kiss to my mate's temple, and she turned her lips toward me, kissing me lightly.

The baby picked that moment to kick, hard. Her belly dipped, and her cookie fell onto the couch.

There was a moment of silence before we all busted up laughing.

"See, the table is overrated," Sienna teased Love.

I pulled my mate closer, and she settled against me, knowing she belonged there.

Life was fucking perfect.

This book was supposed to be longer.
I tried to convince the characters of that—I really did! But I couldn't put them through any more drama than they were already dealing with, so it became a novella.
Some love stories are just simple, I guess. And I think that's kind of beautiful.
Anyway, I hope you loved this final Wildwood story! I have a few more ideas floating around in my head for characters that were mentioned, but I don't know if I'll ever get around to writing them.
My next series will take us back to Scale Ridge, to meet some hunky dragon guys and the ladies fate (cough cough, me) picks out for them! It's called Mate Mountain, and book 1 is Never Fall for a Dragon.
If you haven't read my Deceit & Devotion series yet, it's set in this same world, in case you're looking for more fun and steam!

As always, thank you so much for reading!
All the love,
Lola Glass <3

stay in touch

If you want to receive Lola's newsletter for new releases (no spam!) use this link:

LINK

Or find her on:
FACEBOOK
TIKTOK
INSTAGRAM
PINTEREST
GOODREADS

all series by lola glass

Check out Lola's website for a guide to which of her series are connected!

https://www.authorlolaglass.com/where-do-i-start

Standalones:

Mate Mountain

Wildwood

Deceit & Devotion

Claimed by the Wolf

Forbidden Mates

Wild Hunt

Kings of Disaster

Night's Curse

Outcast Pack

Feral Pack

Mate Hunt

Series:

Burning Kingdom

Sacrificed to the Fae King

Shifter Queen

Wolfsbane

Shifter City

Supernatural Underworld

Moon of the Monsters

Rejected Mate Refuge